Alexander
and Alestria

ALSO BY SHAN SA

The Poems of Yan Ni (poems)

The Red Dragonfly (poems)

Snow (poems)

May the Spring Return (essays)

Porte de la Paix Céleste (novel)

Les Quatre Vies du Saule (novel)

Le Vent Vif et le Glaive Rapide (poems)

The Girl Who Played Go (novel)

Le Miroir du Calligraphe (poems and paintings)

Empress (novel)

Les Conspirateurs (novel)

Alexander
and Alestria

A NOVEL

 Shan Sa

TRANSLATED BY
ADRIANA HUNTER

HARPER
An Imprint of HarperCollins*Publishers*
www.harpercollins.com

ALEXANDER AND ALESTRIA. Copyright © 2008 by Shan Sa. All rights reserved. Printed in the United States of America. No part of this book may be used or reproduced in any manner whatsoever without written permission except in the case of brief quotations embodied in critical articles and reviews. For information, address HarperCollins Publishers, 10 East 53rd Street, New York, NY 10022.

HarperCollins books may be purchased for educational, business, or sales promotional use. For information, please write: Special Markets Department, HarperCollins Publishers, 10 East 53rd Street, New York, NY 10022.

FIRST EDITION

Designed by Leah Carlson-Stanisic

Library of Congress Cataloging-in-Publication Data is available upon request.

ISBN: 978-0-06-154354-8

08 09 10 11 12 ID/RRD 10 9 8 7 6 5 4 3 2 1

You are the flame of this unfinished life
You are the glory of an invincible warrior

SHAN SA

Alexander
and Alestria

CHAPTER I

I, Alexander of Macedonia, son of Philip, king of kings, conqueror of the Greeks, came into this world on the night of a great fire.

The temple of Artemis was alight. Ocher and yellow flames, forests of sparks and twisting wreaths of smoke, spilled into the sky. Thick clouds settled on villages in which every soul had taken refuge indoors, terrified by the fury of the divine huntress.

By the time of my first memory I can already run to the top of the hill. My mother, who dresses me as a girl, takes me to play among the ruins. There are fragments of burned stone scattered in the grass, and wild flowers exhale their bitter fragrance. Wearing a white tunic and sandals with golden straps and with my hair in braids, I stumble up a collapsed flight of steps, hide behind a fallen column, and laugh when the slaves walk past without seeing me. My mother watches me. She tells me of a great temple wiped out by fire, and warns that fire alone is indestructible.

As an adolescent I went back to that hill where the ruins, in turn, had disappeared. A new temple had been built with painted columns, and frescoes along the pediment and arches. My father tells me that Artemis and Apollo were twins. Artemis was born first, already clothed and armed, and she helped her mother bring Apollo into the world. Horrified by the suffering of childbirth, she made a vow of chastity. My father chose to dedicate the new temple to Apollo because, he claimed, my birth had brought an end to the inconsistent world of the moon, of poetic virgins and wandering bacchantes. With me came the era of the sun, of conquerors and lovers devoted to the rages of war.

· · ·

I, ALEXANDER, WHOSE name means male succor and the protection of warriors, was born prince of a kingdom of peasants and soldiers. My father, Philip, sent gifts and silver to families that brought boys into the world. He took care of the boys' physical education and put them in training as soon as they were six. Royal envoys scoured the villages once a year during the celebrations dedicated to Zeus, selecting the tallest, strongest, and most deft boy children to turn them into the best warriors on earth.

Having a soldier in the family was an honor. Every Macedonian household had at least one. Parents whose son had just enlisted in the army and who were losing a pair of hands to work in the fields were handsomely compensated by my father. He promised them the unimaginable spoils of conquered cities. He turned war into an opportunity for everyone to grow rich.

Money and strength were then but one. There was nothing we valued more highly than a man's strength. The Macedonians had been trading on their valor and military expertise for a long time, and neighboring cities paid them to fight their enemies and die for them. My father brought an end to this bartering. He explained to our soldiers that they could not put a price on a Macedonian's life and that selling our strength was wasting a valuable resource.

At the time of my birth our people was fighting for riches and my father for power. The divisions among the Greeks played into my father's hands, and he asserted his authority over everyone as Agamemnon had in the days of Troy. He reigned over the Athenians, the Thebans, and the Spartans while all around him men and women schemed to take his place. During her pregnancy my mother constantly hid herself, convinced that people wanted Philip to have no heir.

I, Alexander, son of Philip, king of the Macedonians, and Olympias, daughter of the king of Epirus, I, descendant of Achilles and Zeus, came into this world in a poor village, close to the temple of Artemis. Apollo is my god and protector.

· · ·

MACEDONIA, MY COUNTRY, I was born for your high mountains and deep valleys. I grew strong in your forests and meadows. Soon I was running to join in the Feast of Horses and babbling the word "horse," which lends itself to so many expressions of strength and speed. Early in the morning I sat on the balustrade of the terrace at the very top of my white palace, and watched women in brightly colored aprons and red skirts as they drove their flocks toward the hills. Clouds glided across a blue sky, followed by their shifting shadows. I peered at the horizon. The sea was far away, farther than the hazy line lit up by the blazing dawn. Way over there Neptune was blowing into his horn and raising a storm; Achilles was sailing for Troy, city of his demise, which would render him immortal; Ulysses was drifting from one island to another, haunted by the sirens. He too would go down in legend.

My mother came over to me, her long black braid wound round her head, her body draped in a white tunic. She took me in her arms, enveloping me in her perfume. I buried myself in her embrace as avidly as a honeybee looking for nectar in the most beautiful flower in Macedonia. She was young and beautiful, daughter of the gods whose whims she described for me, daughter of the heroes whose capricious acts she whispered to me. Her velvet voice transformed bloody wars into lovers' tiffs, monsters of the abyss into cooing birds. Her gaze lingered in the invisible sea. I watched her smile and grow sad, I watched her weep but was unable to console her. My mother bore a secret in her heart.

I could not understand the obsession men had with war. There was nothing more lovely than soft fabrics, colored stones, and women's laughter. In summer the town seemed to float in the heat. I lay in the shade of orange trees with my head on my mother's stomach. Slaves burned grasses and herbs to drive away insects, and they waved palm fronds to cool me. In winter in this vast terraced palace, my loneliness was equally vast. The empty palace echoed to the sound of my mother's singing. She taught me about the lives of plants and the names of birds. I drank in her words as an infant drinks milk.

Sometimes peasants would bring us injured animals: a bird with a broken wing, a limping dog, an orphaned monkey, snakes, and bees. Olympias healed them, and by her side, they regained their strength.

"When you want to talk to an animal, don't move," she told me. "Don't look at it. Keep your eyes on a nearby plant, a tree, a patch of sky. Forget that you are Alexander. Let the animal's thoughts come to you."

That was a time when I knew more about the language of toads and goats and vipers than the language of men.

. . .

THE MEN ALWAYS came back. Their hurried footsteps, their shouting and hearty laughter, echoed round. The smell of wine and sweat and weapons spread. The door creaked noisily, and my father appeared. I ran behind a drape. His one eye swept over the room, turning me to stone. If Philip was in a good mood, he would grab my legs in his great hands and throw me in the air. If Philip was drunk, he would grab me by the hair and bellow. He would rip my girl's clothes, call me a bastard, and threaten to throw me into the lions' den. My mother came to save me, but Philip heaved me up above his head. His tightly curled hair had a strong animal smell. His shouts reverberated through me so that my whole body shook with fear. He cursed Olympias and her family, swearing he would slit her adulterous throat and bury her bastard child alive. He called her a witch, accused her of plotting against him and wanting to overthrow him. He would only drop me back to the ground once he had made my mother weep and terrorized me.

The warriors took their places as pitchers of wine were carried along the corridors. Whole roast calves on silver trays converged on the feasting hall. There, by torchlight, mouths covered in scars gleamed with grease as they popped olives and grapes. My father sat in pride of place. Beneath his thick fair eyebrows, a flame danced in the heart of his one blue eye. He held forth about military operations yet to be perpetrated and kingdoms yet to be conquered. I hid behind a column and listened, fascinated by his booming voice but not understanding a word. The clamor was deafening. Philip poured wine down his throat with one hand and delved into the belly of a roast calf with the other. He drank quickly and ate too much. Pleasure—that sweet, slow progressive sensation—was unknown to him. He liked only instant gratifications so that he could move on to the next.

When the servant women found me, they took me away forcibly and shut me in my room. I leaned on the windowsill, watching lights twinkling around the town. All of Pella was feasting with the king. When the moon was bright I could see naked men walking through the gardens and terraces. They chased each other through the grass and disappeared into the trees. One day the slaves forgot to block my door, and I slipped out of my room. I came round a bend in a corridor and saw Philip almost naked. He was fighting with a young man. They were both groaning. I froze at the sight of them. Fascinated by their thighs and stomachs, I could not tear my eyes away. My father gave long rasping moans that terrified me. I ran to my room in tears and hid under the bed.

The tyrant disappeared for months at a time. Life settled back into its gentle music. I did not want to be a man, to be like

Philip. I liked braids and women's clothes, and learned the disciplines I enjoyed: dance, the lute, poetry, the game of marbles. But the tyrant returned more fiery and brutal, more drunk than ever. Olympias wept. Philip bellowed. I trembled, closing my eyes and blocking my ears. My father's imprecations and my mother's screams as he struck her hammered through my head.

Olympias, your beauty and your origins bewitched Philip. He had your father assassinated and abducted you from your country! Philip the tyrant is not my father. A young Greek warrior loved you, and you conceived me. Olympias, don't cry! I will have our revenge.

. . .

WHEN I REACHED the age of six, my father stole me from my mother. I was driven out of town in a cart and was interned at the Royal School, where I was to learn to fight like every Macedonian man. Still haunted by Olympias's sobs, I walked timidly through that imposing portico. The sons of generals and noblemen kept their distance, eyeing me coldly. I stopped in front of the closest of them. He looked down.

"Are you a girl or a boy?" I asked him.

"A boy," he replied.

"What's your name?"

"Hephaestion."

I liked the way he flushed, the smell of him and his voice. I knew instantly that his friendship would be eternally faithful and protective.

I was the smallest and weakest at school. The boys imitated their fathers' coarse habits and walked with their heads held high.

They made fun of me and deliberately bumped into me. I was flattered merely to exist close to their muscles. I played Olympias, the submissive woman, and charmed them with my affable smiles. I took more interest in the beauty of the male body than in athletic training. The world of boys made me forget the unbearable ugliness of lame, mutilated, blinded, and scarred adults.

Philip announced the imminent arrival of a philosopher famous for his moral rectitude. He wanted the man to come to Pella, he explained, to correct the perversities Olympias had instilled in me. Aristotle appeared one spring morning, dressed in a white tunic which left his thin bony arms uncovered. I hid behind an olive tree, refusing to talk to this man who wanted to educate me in keeping with Greek customs. He would find out about my conversations with birds and my girlish ways. He would punish me and torture me. He was here to work on my reason.

Aristotle sat on a bench and called for Alexander. Hephaestion dragged me by the hand, then pushed me forcibly. I stood in front of the philosopher with my eyes lowered and my hands behind my back, staring at a column of ants carrying grain toward some bushes. Aristotle's voice rang out. It was the first time I had heard pure Greek, unhampered by any accent.

"Macedonia is just one star in a sky full of stars, do you know that?"

I looked up.

Aristotle drew me in and tamed me with his beautiful words and his soothing presence. He let me feel his body, which was nothing like those of the warriors I grew up with. His status as a philosopher meant he could dispense with all athletic training: his skin was soft, his belly fat, his chest flabby. Aristotle was living proof of the diversity of the world. Other men may be as power-ful as warriors. Other towns may be more beautiful than Pella.

In the shade beneath the porticoes Aristotle unrolled his maps. He took an olive branch and traced the roads and shorelines. Country by country, he communicated his passion for geography to me. He smelled good, and his face glowed. No one before him had that phrasing, that way with words, that stringency and clarity. Aristotle was a mason who knew how to build minds. He consolidated the foundations laid down by Olympias, and erected the columns. Mathematics, logic, and metaphysics supported the structure of thought. I grasped that history was not written only by the gods of Olympus or by heroes destined for great exploits. The earth was populated not only with Cerberuses, centaurs, and mermaids. Men had created kingdoms, cities, and governments. Somewhere beyond incantations and witchcraft there was grammar, analysis, and morality. Beyond the art of divination, there was arithmetic, and that quest for a just medium between the failings and qualities of all things, that balancing act, that is called politics.

. . .

PHALANXES OF THE Macedonian army made the very earth tremble. My father advanced at the head of this swaying forest of lances, and never retreated. He returned to Pella only for major feast days. Crowned with laurels and wearing sandals of woven gold, he dominated the world as Zeus did Mount Olympus. His hair was bleached by the sun, his wind-burnished skin obscured by a beard, while his white tunic revealed one shoulder and showed off an arm with bulging muscles scored with lance wounds. And this mighty king publicly ridiculed me: he said I was as thin and stupid as a girl. He grabbed my hand and laid it on his scars, claiming he would teach me about manliness and valor.

Orgies could no longer satisfy his thirst for gratification. He took to keeping lions and releasing captives into the arena with them. The monsters roared and leaped onto these near-naked men. Rare were the slaves who could hold on to their weapons and fight against the lionesses, who were even fiercer than their mates. My father would laugh, standing up and craning his neck when a belly was ripped open. I sat beside him, no longer shaking. Olympias had taught me not to be afraid. She told me that when the storm was in full swing, I had to stay calm and keep my feet on the ground. Because nothing can sway the ground, nothing could destroy it. It is the source of all strength. That was the secret of our ancestor Achilles, who was invincible so long as his feet touched the ground. The spectacle was drawing to a close; my father spat, put his hand through my hair, and waggled my head, roaring with laughter. The sun was setting and the feasting began. The king was soon drunk, and his affection toward me turned to rage. He brandished his goblet and his sword, called me a bastard before everyone, and asked in a booming voice who my father was. The warriors laughed, each claiming I was his daughter.

I had grown up. I no longer cried. I was training myself to withstand suffering. One day a slave would kill the lions. One day Alexander would slay the tyrant.

Having abused her body and debased her soul, Philip neglected the queen who no longer appealed to him. Freed from his pestering attentions, Olympias took refuge in the consolation of women and formed an attachment with a young slave girl she kept in her bedchamber. Olivia was gentle and fair-skinned. When she brushed her garnet lips over my mother's face, she made her forget this life of imprisonment she had never chosen.

One day when he was drunk, the king came across Olivia in the garden and raped her. Bleeding and ashamed, the slave girl drowned herself in a lake. Olympias was demented with grief, resentment, and hatred. She beat her breast, tore out her hair, and cursed the king. She ran barefoot to the top of the ramparts and wanted to throw herself to her death, but the soldiers held her back. The king ordered her to be locked up, and a rumor spread that the queen had gone mad.

I came back from the Royal School for her sake, kneeling before her and calling to her. She did not recognize me but gabbled deliriously, her hair awry and her tunic soiled. I lay my hand on her forehead; she shivered and tried to fight me off. I did not move away but sent her my thoughts through the palm of my hand. A spark appeared in her eyes, and tears sprang up. I drew her to me, and she followed me out of that underground dungeon. She went back to her chamber and lay on the bed where Olivia would no longer join her. Olympias huddled close to me, her tears falling on my breast, but the pain was more bearable now. My muscles were beginning to forge themselves, I had learned to fight with a sword and had my first scar. I no longer knew pity.

Why suffer? Why take pleasure? Why do women and children cry? Why do men get drunk and copulate?

When I asked these questions of Aristotle, he gave me no answers. It was a hot, starless night full of perfumes and the hum of insects.

"You are the star in this starless universe," Aristotle told me.

"You are black, red, yellow, green, purple, white, and blue, the seven colors the Demiurge used to create the world of stars."

I opened my eyes wide and saw mysterious lights in the sky: creatures like butterflies, fireflies, birds, sometimes transparent, sometimes opaque, decked in sparks of light. They brushed past me, settled on my shoulder, then flew away.

My father wanted to make a warrior of me. My mother claimed that I was the son of a god. Aristotle hoped to make a good and just ruler of me. I wanted to become none of these three Alexanders.

Papyrus books had taught me about the pyramids, the Sphinx, and boats with crimson sails. I believed I was destined for oceans and deserts, for forests, mountains, and volcanoes.

Without Homer, the exploits of men would have been scattered on the wind. Without him, kings would not have known immortality. I, Alexander, would give birth to majestic landscapes, grandiose cities, and warriors who exceeded all norms. Their weapons would be exceptional, their horses magnificent, their words unparalleled. Riding forth with furious desire, they would know neither hunger nor thirst, forget rumor and calumny, and ignore the countries and hearts trampled by their steeds. They would conquer the sun. They would steal and compete with each other to advance faster, ever faster, to the very edge of the universe.

I would be a poet.

. . .

MY BODY WAS changing and causing me suffering. Standing naked beside the river, I was intimidated by the soldiers who stopped their horseplay under the waterfall to turn and look at me. I was no longer slender as a little girl: my shoulders, hips, and buttocks were muscled up by Olympian exercises. The brown and black curls of my hair floated about my face, which had lost its childish curves. I threw myself into the water to hide. Hephaestion came over and whispered that the commander of the phalanx had asked us to take part in a water fight. I was overcome with shame and indignation, and escaped by swimming downstream. Rushes swayed in the wind, swifts skimmed over the water and flitted up to the trees. There was an inexpressible pain inside me: something was about to happen, and I knew it would bring both fear and joy.

Hephaestion always watched me, growing aggressive when I spoke to other boys. He sulked for days on end, then came back. The tall, brutish adolescents at the school had stopped making fun of me, looking for opportunities to flatter me and allow me to win wrestling matches. In exchange for this servitude they took turns asking me to scrub their backs when bathing. Only Crateros continued to assault me, never hesitating to spit in my face or hurt me in combat. His hostility appalled me: I hovered around him, smiling at him and flashing him burning glances, which infuriated Hephaestion. The two boys fought over everything and anything; they even went so far as to brandish their swords and threaten to kill each other. I leaned against a column and watched them with a feeling of melancholy.

I was beautiful, I realized that. Not like these boys born for massacres; I had only my beauty to protect me and to ensure I was accepted by other men. I wanted to please everyone I met. Pleasing is a means of escape, it is a means of domination.

I realized how much I had changed when I walked out to meet Philip on his return to Pella after yet another victory: the tyrant watched me in silence. At the banquet he seated me beside him and covered me with compliments. He called for Bucephalus, a huge horse with a dazzling white coat, and offered him to me.

He ordered me to pose naked before the royal sculptors. In their deft hands, the clay became a mouth, curls, a torso, thighs. The divine Apollo and I were now but one. Together we would dictate the law of perfection throughout Macedonia and Greece. Philip came to watch, walked round, then left. He came back and stood before the statue, motionless as he contemplated it.

He begged me to let him kiss me, ordered me to open my arms to him. He clambered over me suffocatingly, kneeling before me when I rebuffed him with a scream. My rejection unleashed his desire: his gifts piled up, he summoned me to every celebration, introducing me as the future king of Macedonia, seating me in pride of place beside him, pouring wine for me as eagerly as a woman in love.

His efforts flattered and disgusted me. His passion softened my loathing even as it heightened it. I nurtured a towering contempt for the human body and for those obsessed with the flesh. A new Alexander was burgeoning within me. I could not tell whether he was strong or weak. He told me that my beauty was the rarest of goods: if I learned how to barter, I would become a superior being.

Everything was reduced to trade-offs. I gave only on condition of receiving. Philip, the king who was never refused anything, began to enjoy this game that reversed our roles. I had become his tyrant; he reveled in his servitude. To persuade me to undress, he had to heap gifts at my feet: gold plates, weapons, jewels, all the treasures he had grasped from the Greeks by force and by blood, at the risk of his own life. I soon tired of this accumulation; gold elicited only my disdain. My displeasure aroused him further, and he made dogged attempts to earn my smile.

I asked for every extravagant gift that came to mind: a three-horned bull, an embalmed Egyptian, a shrunken head, a freshly aborted fetus from a slave girl. When I tired of the game and felt satisfied with my offerings, like Apollo consenting to step down from the heavens, I gave myself to him and his companions in pleasure with perfect indifference. He would laugh and put his golden laurel wreath on my head, offering me his throne in exchange for one long kiss. Through all the madness of this capricious behavior, I kept my feet anchored to the ground.

Of all the things he had, I wanted only his strength.

．　．　．

EVER IN PURSUIT of the model of divine beauty, artists abandoned the coarse bodies of athletes and became infatuated with the cool contours of my muscles, my graceful limbs and fine features.

Looking at my reflection, I no longer saw the timid girl with braided hair, or the melancholy little boy who dreamed of being Homer. Instead there was a young prince with a proud nose and a determined chin. He had large, green innocent eyes that fascinated the powerful Macedonian warriors, and an adolescent mouth that the Greeks longed to kiss. His square shoulders, strong chest, and narrow waist, his firm belly and muscled buttocks, still had the harmonious curves and sweet proportions of a woman. I had become a work of art and was offered to everyone, but was forever inaccessible to common mortals.

How could it be that such filth and crime had made my body so resplendent? I was obsessed with hatred, ravaged by vengeance, initiated in the art of torture, unmoved by corpses, laughing as I decapitated and eviscerated them . . . how could it be that my features were still so incomparably pure?

Is the face a comedian's mask hiding the tragedy of the soul?

The body a statue of marble to serve men and the gods?

With Aristotle, I was an assiduous and intelligent pupil. With my father, a torturer and a whore. With my fellow students, a tyrannical leader and a servile lover. With Hephaestion, a suspicious woman, constantly haranguing him reproachfully to make him suffer.

I had grown accustomed to being several different people. There were as many Alexanders as there were men and women interested in me, in love with me, intoxicated by my face.

Paris took Helen away, and the Greeks waged war on the Trojans for ten years. Achilles killed Hector and was killed in turn. The defeated Priam had his throat cut, and the conquering Agamemnon was assassinated by his own wife. Beauty is prey to strength. Beauty destroys strength. From a crawling caterpillar I had turned into a butterfly. From the defenseless little girl I had forged my own strategy. My beauty had subjugated Philip; it had incited young men to fight each other, and elicited vows of loyalty. It made Hephaestion weep and tricked Aristotle. I offered it, then took it back; I threw it out, then hid it again. Beauty was my sword, and I loathed it.

Hatred of beauty was my armor. Self-loathing appeased my pain.

Philip had taught me to spy, Olympias to plot and scheme. I never hesitated to follow the king's order in killing lovers he thought were traitors. I trained myself to know no pity in order to protect my girlish heart and my poet's dreams.

I woke in the mornings exhausted by my restless sleep. I stripped naked and posed for artists who displayed my image as the aesthetic ideal to every nation. I would rule over this world of ugliness and violence with my radiant smile and innocent expression. In Pella everyone had become my lover, my slave. Everyone wanted to die within me, had sworn to die for me.

My mother's indulgence and constant weeping exasperated me. I now hated her more than I loathed Philip. So long as she was alive, her existence would remind me that I was the instrument she had forged to spite the tyrant. Wherever I was, she would be inside my head, whispering her disappointment and resentment toward men. My mother was the mirror in which I contemplated my own reflection in horror.

Who was I?

A weakling or a towering force?

.   .   .

HEPHAESTION, DO YOU remember our early years spent running through the forests like fawns?

Do you remember our first embrace?

Do you remember the sunbeam that came in through the temple doors, unfurling a great carpet of light at our feet!

Veiled in brilliant red by the setting sun and draped in white cloth, you blushed and smiled, twisting your head away when I tried to kiss you. I pinned you to the plinth at Apollo's feet, reached out my hand, and let your tunic slip from your shoulder. As you struggled, you did the same to me so that I was naked. You were only fifteen years old, and I even younger. Do you know that I was already accustomed to hairy adult bodies and was moved by your young, hairless skin? Your lips seemed to swell, your eyes pierced mine, paralyzing me. I had to force you to turn round. You clung to Achilles' ankles. Drops of water fell on my arms, you wept as you gave me my first climax.

You have always asked me why I wept with you that day. And why I laughed as I wept. Here is my secret: I was my father's whore. I had just freely given you what my father paid for in cattle, horses, and gold pieces. I had just realized that what you had given me without compensation was worth more than the treasures of every Greek city. I learned that there was something in the world, a feeling that could not be bartered, stolen, or taken by force.

Love repairs what beauty destroys. I became a man the day you gave yourself. I, who hoped to find a warrior to release me from the prison created by my father, I nurtured the desire to become a hero to guard our purity!

Hephaestion, do you remember? For the first year of school I was always on the ground during wrestling classes. The boys called me a bastard and you fought for me, rolling on the ground with Crateros, who took pleasure in humiliating me. Do you know that for a long time I wondered which I liked best: you, my protector who looked on me tenderly, or him, the cruel one who rejected me?

When we left the temple, the sun was shining along the path. I was filled with the happiness of having known physical delight. As I walked hand in hand with you, I understood that I was no longer the king's slave, and now I wanted to become king, your king and king of the Macedonians and the Greeks. On that day I knew I had something more than my father, the invincible warrior, ever had.

I am woman and man. I am stronger, more intelligent, and more determined than a man who has not known a woman's suffering.

Be thanked, Hephaestion, for your patience and tolerance. I was once afraid you might abandon me, and I tormented you to keep you by my side. This evening I release you from my possessive desire. You are free.

Tomorrow Philip will die, or he will survive.

Tomorrow I shall be king, or I shall be condemned.

Tomorrow will be ours, or we shall be forgotten to the world for ever.

Come, Hephaestion! Let us join Cassander, Crateros, Perdiccas, and the others. We should not make them wait.

Slaves, light the braziers! Dionysus, break open your pitchers, let the wine flow.

Let us drink and make love and celebrate!

Here's to us, brothers in arms, children of Macedonia, may we conquer pyramids, deserts, oceans, the steepest mountains and the most magnificent cities.

Blood is our strength; pain our ecstasy!

· · ·

PAUSANIAS DID NOT break his word; his dagger struck Philip.

The king crawled along the ground before falling motionless. Only his hands still quivered. Blood blossomed on his white tunic, tinting it red. All around me women screamed and children howled. Men blamed themselves and beat their chests. They tore their clothes and lost their sandals as they barged past each other in pursuit of the murderer. Olympias threw herself at my feet, shaking me as she sobbed. I looked up toward the sun and let tears of joy stream over my cheeks.

Aristotle, your words hardened the ribs of my flanks, your lessons straightened my spine! Your knowledge armed my mind. Henceforth I shall be a king, I shall dominate this world of violence with the strength of thought. Pausanias was a soldier prepared to die for a great cause; others will follow his example and die for Alexander.

I am not the son of Philip, I am the son of a god. Apollo forged me in his divine brazier to make an indestructible warrior of me. Now that its wings have grown, the firebird is ready to fly. It will launch itself toward heights unknown to man, where there are dangers, challenges, and infinity.

.   .   .

ALEXANDER REJECTED SUGGESTED negotiations. Alexander wanted to show the world how determined he was to reign. Alexander repudiated Aristotle, whose talk was of clemency. Rebellious cities would be reconquered with the lance.

Thebes, the ancient white city backed up against the sea, the city of trade and giant sailing ships, Thebes, the home of prophetesses and fallen gods, Thebes waited for us with its gates closed and its ramparts defended by mercenary archers who had run to its aid from neighboring towns. I feigned hesitation, sent messages to Pella, called for the most astute diplomats to begin talks. As I anticipated, in council these traitors could not wait to communicate the good news to the Thebans. I waited twenty-one days for their hope of peace to disarm their vigilance.

The order to attack was given in the middle of a moonless night. The cavalry advanced on horses whose hooves were wrapped in cloth. The infantrymen left their lances behind and marched in silence, saber in hand. It was only when we reached the walls of Thebes that I called for the drum to be sounded. Thebes woke too late. Behind me my soldiers formed great waves that spilled into the city. Swords flashed zigzags in the dark. Arrows whistled. War cries mingled with wailing from the injured. The smell of blood and the thrum of combat made me deaf and blind to danger. I kept on advancing, not noticing those who fell beside me and would never again see the light of day. The gates creaked open noisily and my cavalry streamed in. The Macedonians had orders to pursue any resistance, even into the Thebans' beds. The massacre lasted three days. Street after street, house after house, my soldiers killed, pillaged, and raped. Sword in one hand, a glass of wine in the other, I amused myself slicing and dismembering bodies. I dined while noblemen were grilled alive beneath the steps. Rather than soothing my rage, victory increased it tenfold.

I left Thebes dissatisfied and melancholy, riding at the head of my army, followed by the women and children taken as slaves. Thebes was in flames. Thebes was reduced to columns of black smoke.

Citizens of Greece, listen! There are none more wily than the Thebans. There are no ramparts more impregnable than theirs. There is no history more proud than theirs. Philip conquered them. Alexander destroyed them. Submit now, why wait! The Macedonian king is on his way! His lance brings with it lightning and his sword brings forth fire. When his mount Bucephalus whinnies, the swiftest steeds are paralyzed. Flee! Run! Crawl! Alexander is on his way, for peace or for annihilation!

. . .

FEROCITY AND INTRANSIGENCE are necessities. In order to be feared, a military commander must prove he is not afraid to have men mutilated and put to death. He must sacrifice his peace of mind for his authority. I no longer drank wine until it had been tasted by a slave. I woke in the night believing an assassin had crept into my tent. Philip came to me in my dreams, covered in blood and crawling along the ground, clutching at me with his icy hands. This was my punishment for plotting against my father.

I returned to Pella. With my white tunic, a gold laurel wreath on my forehead, and the royal scepter against my heart, I arrived through the principal gateway, cheered as Philip once was. Olympias took me in her arms. Her woman's perfume erased the ashen faces, the wounds seething with maggots, and the burned corpses. My mother's voice woke me from my nightmares. I noticed olive trees again, and orange blossom, sparkling water in the fountains and the gentle hum of a peaceful life: doves cooing, sparrows scrapping in the trees, bell-ringing carried on the wind, the clinking sounds of masons building a house, the laughter of Macedonians cleaning their linen down by the river.

My wounds scarred over, and I regained my strength. Pella became unbearable to me once again. Rumors circulated through doors and open windows in the palace: the world still thought of me as a bastard, as Olympias's daughter clinging to the tunic of a mother who had murdered her own husband. They said I was under her spell, they whispered that she poisoned anyone who questioned my legitimacy, and they laughed at this weak Alexander who let himself be manipulated by his debauched, scheming mother.

I set off for war again to escape the wagging tongues. Far from Pella I could make use of my mother's devotion. Orders were sent to her in secret: she had to eliminate anyone who contested my actions; she had to continue wreaking my revenge on Philip, silencing those who sang his praises, wiping away every trace of his legend, washing clean the marble floors and columns impregnated with his smell. She had to help me drive him out of my life and erase him from my memory.

Battle after battle, my soldiers grew richer and I accumulated experience as well as maps and books expounding the wonders of this world. The fury of a body streaming with blood and sweat alternated with the chill lucidity of solitary thought, constructing strategies. I was overcome with melancholy as soon as the exultant rage abated. Athens fell without a fight: that metropolis which once teemed with traders, sailors, politicians, and philosophers was now reduced to ruins. The agora was deserted, but the taverns prospered: the poorest boys and girls went there to prostitute themselves and sell their souls.

Sitting at the foot of the Acropolis, I was before the very gates of eternity, looking toward the horizon: the sea, silvery waves, and sailing boats. Socrates had been condemned to poisoning. Plato's republic was now a mere shadow on the walls of a cave. Athens and its ruined palaces, the great city of Thebes that I myself burned down, and Macedonia, a land rich in cereal crops but poor in the arts: these three formed a vast prison locking me in its unhealthy backstreets and decadent ways.

Disguised as a soldier, I loitered around the port of Athens looking for easy pleasures. Boys hovered round me, flashing me looks and tugging at my arm. The most beautiful succeeded in getting me to sit down and share their cheap wine. The sun was setting over the sea and the clouds turning scarlet. Growing steadily more drunk as my frustration grew, I could not find a single face that attracted me, a body that smelled good, a person who could bring me gratification to distract me from my gloom. I turned a street corner and caught the eye of a frightened little boy selling dates under a tree. Inexplicably, my body was inflamed by him. I grabbed him and, despite his pleading and crying, dragged him to the nearest inn and emptied myself into him.

The following morning I left Athens as soon as the sun was up, horrified by the memory of that drunken night, by the little boy's terrified expression—so like Alexander's as a child. I had committed Philip's crime. His soul was distilled in my blood. In death, he lived through me, making a mockery of my pointless rebellion.

I needed greater acts of cruelty, fiercer battles! I had to gallop and climb and throw myself at the highest battlements. Only arrows and the sparking clash of swords, only the cries of dying men and the flames of burning cities, could exorcise my anguish! With Greek cities pacified, the world had become too small to contain my suffering, which prospered more swiftly than my pleasure. I needed new cities, barbarian nations, and unknown lands to deflate my pain.

Persia, its infinite expanse and shadowy provinces, appeared like a dream, a necessary dream and an indispensable challenge. It became the obsession that promised to bring an end to my torment.

Ambition healed and intoxicated me. I had no choice: in a long starless night, Alexander would be a shooting star, burning intensely. Though short, his life would leave the memory of its swift dazzling trajectory across the celestial vault.

. . .

OLYMPIAS TALKED TO me of marriage. I knew from my men that she had started looking for a wife for me among the daughters of Macedonian noblemen. Her dreams of a happy marriage and her longing to be a grandmother made the very air in the palace difficult to breathe. I tried to evade the question with talk of my father, accusing my mother of allowing him to pervert me, and of tolerating my vices as she had his. Olympias looked at me, her eyes filled with sadness.

"Woman!" I screamed, "you gave me love, but that love nurtured a monster. I don't want to be married! I don't want a wife like you! I don't want to have children I can harm!"

She looked away and said nothing.

I grabbed her by the shoulders and gave full vent to my anger.

"Look at me," I bellowed, shaking her. "I'm not the man you think you love. I'm not a god. I destroy cities for the sheer pleasure of showing that I'm more fierce and dangerous than Philip, to exceed him in every crime he committed. I have decapitated children, eviscerated women, burned men alive when they have done me no harm at all. Oh, Olympias, you gave birth to a tyrant!"

She held me in her arms and wept.

"Give me a child," she whispered. "Then go and never come back! If I raise a son of yours, he will be a good and just king, he will be wise and clement . . ."

Her words touched my heart, which had no armor against her. My tears mingled with hers, and we wept together for our ruined lives. Night fell, and Olympias sang me the same songs that had lulled my childhood. I lay with my head on her stomach and fell asleep as I used to then.

Women are stronger than men. Even Philip, despite his drunken rages, had never succeeded in defeating Olympias. How could I escape her will? I set off on horseback again, leaving her in charge of the palace and the scheming trappings of power. But her letters followed me beyond mountains; her voice silenced the tumult of war and brought me back by her side, in her bedchamber looking out over orange trees and fountains. I could not help myself replying, and our exchanges were like butterflies flitting over fields strewn with corpses. She and I were harnessed together by the timeless link that joins a man and a woman. Philip was dead; I in turn had become her intrepid warrior, her devouring force, her hand reaching out to expand its territories over the world. She was my home; she had the keys to my treasure and watched fiercely over Pella. I waged war at the front, and she pacified to the rear. I pillaged, and she balanced the accounts. I killed, and she dressed the wounds.

How to fight a woman who had borne suffering, accepted violence, survived brutality? There was a small room in the palace where black crystals were laid out on an altar. My mother shut herself away in there, and no one, not even Philip, had ever dared open that door. Olympias knew everything about me; I had been a part of her. I knew nothing of her, nothing except the mountainous land she came from, a place where people wore black and went to market to sell scorpions, snakes, spiders, and precious stones with magic powers and evil promises. The men practiced vengeance as others might sing and dance. The women of her family, promised to Dionysus by an ancestral pact, learned from him the skill to subdue warriors.

Preparations for a military expedition against the Persians had begun many years before. Philip had reformed our armies to make them more mobile. With archers marching ahead of the phalanxes and walls of lances hiding the cavalry, our square formations could transform themselves into curved lines at any moment. After good harvests and with our grain stores full, the mention of a war against the Persians motivated Greek cities that had once submitted in terror: they regained their dignity and aspired to a sense of unity. Meanwhile, Olympias had taken several lovers, and she hid behind them, governing from the shadows, the intrigues of one group neutralizing those of another. I was no longer afraid my throne would be usurped.

I introduced more rigor and discipline to Philip's army. I studied maps of roads and gathered useful information. I knew the names of influential ministers and eunuchs. I knew exactly where the favorite of Darius, the Great King, had a beauty spot. Knowledge paralyzes action. The more I learned, the more I real-

ized how little I knew of an empire a thousand times more powerful than mine. Days passed, and still I made no decision. It was
Olympias who hastened my departure. Knowing that she could
not hold me back, she harassed me day and night about taking a
wife. Her muttering about the continuity of our dynasty infuriated me. Her mournful silence disarmed my rage. She made my
life unbearable.

One night in a dream I saw my queen. She lived in a temple
built on the pinnacle of a rock. Dressed in fiery red, she stood
in the first row of a group of young girls all in white. She wore
a necklace of Byzantine gold and scarlet pearls from some rich,
unknown land. She was reaching up to the heavens, and a slow,
reverberating chorus rang out, praising the glories of some unfamiliar god. Like water flowing over burning embers, her song
soothed my fevered soul.

When I woke, my sense of wonder turned to doubt. Plato
taught that each of us is part of a celestial entity that breaks in
two as it falls to earth, thus beginning the quest for love. Without a doubt, this princess was mine as I was hers. Where was that
rock? Did she know I even existed, that I had seen her, that I already loved her even before I knew her? Was she waiting for me?
Had she seen me? Had she dreamed of me? Would she commit
the terrible mistake of binding herself to another soul?

I announced my imminent departure to Olympias. Her eyes
shrouded themselves with tears.

"No one can challenge the barbarian empire," she murmured.
"Our men will be no more than droplets of water spilled along a
shoreline. They will all be absorbed and erased."

It was not in pursuit of victory that I wanted to confront

danger! Tired of accusing him, I wearily cited Philip once more:

"My father failed; I must carry on."

"Your father did not fail. He was a thoughtful king. He listened to Zeus and managed to avoid disaster."

Hearing her speak well of Philip infuriated me.

"I'm not a man of reason," I said, raising my voice. "I will go beyond where my ancestor Achilles fell. The gods on Olympus didn't choose Philip to bear their glory. I am the chosen one! I am the son of Apollo, and Artemis drew me from your belly, that's why she let her temple burn the night I was born. There's no point in discouraging me; I shall reach the ramparts of Babylon."

"You would rather challenge the power of foreign gods than govern," she said menacingly. "I never succeeded in stopping your father, and I won't be able to stop you. I shall lose you. Your heart will forget me and I shall die alone. . . ."

I sighed. "You have done enough intriguing to keep me in this palace. Dry your tears, your king commands it. Being born the wife and mother of warriors is a sad fate. But show yourself worthy of your name. Let me go."

Olympias said nothing. She knew all this was inevitable.

I arranged for Apollo to pronounce a favorable oracle. Speeches were made before council. Never mind the rumors that Alexander wanted to prove to the world that he was not Olympias's daughter. Hephaestion, Perdiccas, Cassander, Crateros, Lysimachus, the lovers of my youth and my longtime companions, cut open their arms and let their blood mingle with mine as an oath of eternal loyalty. In keeping with the treaty of Corinth, all Greek cities sent us their most valiant men.

Horses gleaming, troops roused, our war cries rang out. The

great army set out upon its earthly route. Some detachments set sail by sea, their mission to plague Persian ships and make them believe our allied armies would attack from the coast.

Begone, the gilded prison where Philip locked me away in his glory and his misery. Begone, kisses from Olympias, who wanted me to be her little girl forever. Begone, Macedonia that gave me life, Aristotle and Homer who watched over me as I grew. I, Alexander, am destined for the mysteries of civilization, for the vastness of this world. I run, I gallop, I fly toward the land of the pharaohs.

Open your arms, Osiris and Isis, gods of my rebirth, givers of life and strength, I am coming with my wound and my nightmares.

· · ·

THE HOT WIND blew as I watched the sun sink over the ramparts of Memphis. The wind from the Nile—heavy with the smell of wet earth, of reeds and grilled fish—erased Olympias's perfume and the rustling of her tunic. The sun had not yet disappeared behind the horizon; the moon had already risen, pale, transparent, and round.

My soldiers were preparing for a Macedonian feast day in the encampment but, so far from Pella, it did not have the same gaiety, the same feel. Even though the moon of the pharaohs was more majestic than that which rose over Greek soil, Memphis—a bustling trading city—exhaled the same stench of decadence as Athens. I searched in vain for splendors recorded on papyrus. Time continued to trickle through the hourglass, but the Egyptians already had the weary expression of a kingdom that has lived too long in eternity.

Ammon had supplanted Osiris. The god of the sun demanded exclusive adoration and obedience. I considered it essential to appear at his sanctuary if I was to convince the Egyptians to submit to my authority for any length of time. I was told of a desert stretching as far as the eye could see, of hills of flames and nine-headed vultures. I heard of an army of shades advancing as columns of sand blown by the wind, an army that once destroyed the powerful Persian troops. I knew no fear at all. Dangers merely heightened my will.

Four days wandering through that ocean of dunes, four nights of forced marching beneath the stars, I turned a deaf ear to the soldiers' complaints. The sun burned down on me. I shielded my eyes with straw and saw the waves of sand twisting, breaking, and reforming, but never once did I think of retreating. Retreat would mean forever abandoning the sphinx and the pyramids.

In the heart of the oasis Ammon's guards exhausted me with ritual dancing, chanting, and praises, then they let me into the low-ceilinged hut with its roof of palm fronds. The high priest, decked in jewels and bought with my gold, predicted what I wanted to hear: their god appointed me king of kings. He announced that, with his benediction, Alexander would be invincible among men.

We made the return journey without stopping once. Carried by the uplifting oracle, my soldiers braved the desert in jubilant mood. I slept in the saddle astride Bucephalus. I pictured myself back there, facing the disc of the sun. I had asked this question of the high priest: "Why was I born when the end of the world had already begun?" Taken aback, he sat in silence. I was gripped with the urge to laugh, and left the sanctuary lighthearted. The end of the world had already begun because I was born to burn it down, to destroy it.

On the banks of Lake Mareotis I used the point of my lance to draw out a new city on fallow land. I gave it my name.

Alexandria of Egypt, you shall prosper after this ancient world has perished in flames with me!

CHAPTER 2

They call me Tania. They also call me Talestita. I am tall and slender. I have a pet bird. I gather my hair in two braids and dress in red. I am often seen frowning and thinking—it is what I like best.

Other girls used to make fun of me because I was not happy like them; my body was more fragile. I was the queen's serving girl, and she liked my air of melancholy. She told me I had a more restful presence than the others, who were too playful and chirpy. They all teased me because I have white skin, golden eyes, and fair, curly hair. They laughed and called me "the foreigner" because the elders said I was the daughter of a foreign king and my family had perished in a massacre. A foreigner among girls with dark eyes and black hair, and yet I was the only one my queen trusted as her scribe. I wrote down her words on flat pieces of stone, using tinted water and a reed cut on the diagonal. The ink dried a yellow color for orders and orange for tallies of horses and sheep.

Few people in our tribe could write. We had no books. My mother, a servant to the previous queen, taught me the secrets of written signs. She told me our language had the strength of concentration, and that each of our signs was worth ten words in any other tongue.

In the evenings the queen would lie on the ground and read the stars, telling stories that developed as the stars moved across the sky. She dictated them to me, and I, Tania, wrote them down by the light of a lantern. We hid these pages of stone so the other girls would not find them. The queen told me I should wall up our book in a cave the day she died. At the time I could not know that our lives would be so brief and so intense.

The ink turned white for the stories from the stars.

That year the queen was fifteen years old, in keeping with our customs. I was a little older than her. I may have been melancholy, but I was a stranger to sorrow.

.   .   .

ON THE STEPPES we were known as the Amazons, which meant the tribe of girls who loved horses. We reared the swiftest, hardiest horses with the most magnificent coats. Like other nomads, we strayed beneath the skies in search of tall grass and limpid water. We were tough, solitary girls, forging no links with other peoples. No one knew where we came from; no one knew of our divinity; no one knew the Amazons, who kept the secret of their origins to themselves.

Millions of years earlier our ancestors lived on a luxurious mountain called Siberia where the trees blossomed all summer long. They knew how to tame men and horses, and lived in harmony with nature, but one day nature betrayed them and forced them down from the mountain onto the plain. Our ancestors walked and walked and walked. They walked for decades on end before discovering the fertile steppes.

In those far-off days there was a queen known as the Great Queen. She established the tribe's laws and devised its writing. She observed nature: birds in flight, the intelligence of leaves, flowers opening. Inspired by these moving things that gave life its animation, she invented our written language, which looks sometimes like flowers, sometimes like leaves, sometimes like birds twirling in the sky. The Great Queen was the only woman in our tribe to bear children. There was a tribe on the other face of Mount Siberia and she obtained their king's seed. Before their union the two tribes had never met, for the mountain was almost impassable.

The king managed to cross the treacherous pass and met the Great Queen on a mountain path. The queen, who was in pursuit of a boar, lowered her bow. She had never seen a man like him in her forest. She knew nothing of him, his name, his origins, his race. Devastated by his beauty, she decided to capture him in a net. She brought him back along with his followers, and paraded them before her women like trophies. The king was taller than the men our ancestors used as slaves, and in his nakedness, he glowed like the sun itself.

The queen fostered a terrible longing to couple with him. She bathed him and called for serving girls to massage him. She had him thrown into the middle of her enormous bed, a carpet of the most tender grasses, the most fragrant flowers, and the silkiest feathers. She dressed in a veil stitched with bird scales from a species that has since disappeared but that once dazzled with beams of reflected light. She put a crown on her head, a tall arrangement of tree blossom like an invisible forest reaching up to the skies, and she walked over to him to begin her seduction. Fascinated by such splendor, unlike anything he had ever known, the king made love to her for three days and three nights without interruption.

The queen was so in love that she planted giant bamboo, golden ivy, and venomous flowers around the bed to form a magnificent aviary. She asked the birds to watch over her captive. The queen was so in love that she forgot her duties. She forgot food and drink and the girls of Siberia who wept in her absence. She could think only of her man, of bathing him, suckling him, kissing him, feeding him, and singing him her most beautiful songs. She could not take her eyes off him, or take a single step away from his side. The whole world could have collapsed and she would have had only one regret: her body could not be permanently united with his because they were like two tree trunks with mismatched limbs; their bodies could not fuse into one, as two flowers can never be one.

The king missed his people, and his sadness made the queen unhappy. But she could not abandon her tribe, she could not follow him, for her world was here, with her girls and her animals; this was her land, the land of her ancestors. One morning the queen finally emerged from the aviary to give an audience. It was a very heated gathering: the girls, rebelling against their neglectful queen, called for the foreigner's head. Weighed down by their reproach, the queen had to use all her skills as an orator to calm the women's anger. When she returned to the aviary, she found a gaping hole in the bamboo wall. She understood that the girls had stolen her man and torn out her heart.

She followed footprints along the path to the place they had first met, but the tracks disappeared into the swaying grass. Had he been captured? Had he been assassinated? Haunted by a grim sense of foreboding, the queen kept walking. She called the beautiful creature by the name she had given him. She cried out. The deep valleys gave the only reply, an echo of her sorrow.

The queen no longer wanted to reign. She lay on her bed, now made of dry grass and wilted flowers. She lay there with her eyes trained on the treetops, waiting for her beloved bird to return. The moon rose. The moon set. Still the man was invisible, as if he had never existed.

She was racked with terrible spasms. She writhed and sobbed. For three days and three nights she tried to rip her own belly open, but her servants tied her hand and foot to stop her tearing her own flesh with her nails. On the fourth morning two children came from her belly, already dead. The queen was consumed with pain and bitter disappointment. No one knew whether she had seen her children, no one knew whether she had understood that loving a man was impossible. From that day forward, from generation to generation, our tribe passed down this law: it was forbidden to love the masculine race; it was forbidden to conceive.

Loving a man and bearing his child destroys a girl of Siberia. I, Tania, had received the order from my mother, Tankiasis, to watch over my queen. She carried within her the continuation of our tribe.

. . .

WHAT LAY ON the far side of Mount Siberia?

It was said there was an ocean and seafaring people.

It was said there were huntsmen who lived in trees with golden leaves.

It was said there was a desert covered in sands beautiful and pure as a blend of diamonds and gold.

It was said there were men who killed each other, ate each other, drank the blood of their brothers and sisters, and coupled with their mothers and fathers.

On the far side of Siberia there were as many splendors as there were crimes. Our Great Queen had committed the sin of being with child to one of these men. That was why the God of Ice strangled her children in her belly with their own cord— because the fusion of purity with impurity was impossible.

Hundreds of thousands of years later, eternal snow swept over the mountain. Generation after generation our tribe moved farther from the sky and closer to the earth. On the steppes our ancestors forgot the birds with scaled skin and rainbow-colored feathers, and learned to tame those wingless birds known as horses.

Our tribe began its decline with the Great Queen's sin. We lived in a world where nature was not so generous and animals not so magnificent. Good grazing became sparse, and we had to fight off hordes of horsemen who descended on our flocks. The winters were harsh, with winds that howled more threateningly than the wolves. The swirling snow forced us to shut ourselves into our tents with our sheep.

I knew that the steppes would be our tribe's last kingdom

before it emigrated into the shades. I foresaw the end without sadness, and I let the smell of a new spring intoxicate me. In the summer I closed my eyes and listened to the silence and the rumblings of the steppes. Rain clouds clashed on the horizon and spread across the sky. The wind drove great emerald green waves over the plains. White cranes, frightened by the thunder, danced as if possessed. I sat at the entrance to my tent and watched the lightning throw its terrifying writing across the mauve vault of the sky. The autumn unfurled sapphire blue skies, and I lay in the grass watching butterflies with wings covered in tiny scales.

The other girls made fun of my melancholy ways.

Melancholy is the poetry of a carefree life.

. . .

I, TANIA, SERVING girl to the queen, do not know where I was born; I do not know my age or my birth name. Here, everyone calls me Tania, "the fragrance of butterflies."

"Am I beautiful?" I asked my mother, the one who took me in and fed me on ewe's milk.

"Beauty is a lake that exists within us," she replied. "Beauty is a reflection of the sparkling, transparent Siberian glacier. Beauty is the smile of God."

We, the girls from that snow-covered mountain, we were not afraid of hunger, heat, cold, or invasion. Each of us had a tiny portion of the glacier. As guardians of its white flame, we lived solitary lives, far from cities and kings.

The eagles were our friends: the queen knew how to call them, and they would come down from the skies to act as our guides. We tended our horses, bathing them, rubbing them, and grooming them adoringly. For horses were our faithful companions. The steppes did not have the riches of the mountain; there was very little fruit with soft juicy flesh; the rare red berries that we found made us skip for joy. We hunted with bow and arrow for hares, foxes, and wolves to give us the strength for our mounted expeditions, which could last several months.

Once a year, when we had eaten well and drunk wine made from roots and berries, when our horses were well fed and groomed, we would launch ourselves into a headlong gallop, continuing for many moons without rest. Our bodies were gripped by such frenzy, our souls overcome by such a longing to fly, that we set off for the farthest limits of the steppes, following our queen to the point of exhaustion. We sustained ourselves on thin air, the rain, and the wind. We knew neither sorrow nor fear. We knew only the freedom that was ours and was the source of our pride. We were like migratory birds summoned by a mysterious force. We raced toward the place where the moon rose, heading for the great annual celebrations that drew together all the peoples of the steppes.

Men and women jostled and barged on the banks of the river Iaxarte. Noblemen could be distinguished by their hats of leather or felt, decorated with feathers, flowers, and animal heads. Lowlier people competed in their techniques for tying turbans. Tribes gathered here to exchange weapons, tents, jewels, and women. Everyone spoke a language the nomads used for trading. The girls of our tribe knew a few words of it, but only the queen and I perfectly mastered this dialect of numbers, exclamations, and exaggerations.

During that month of festivities, we exchanged our horses for leather pouches, painted pots, bead necklaces, and young girls. We gleaned information about the huge world beyond the steppe. That was how we learned that Persia, the vastest empire under the sun, had been brought down by an army from the west. Endless battles had sent the Persians fleeing eastward. Their sumptuous fabrics, elegant plates, and jewelry decorated with precious stones were everywhere in our markets and changed hands for almost nothing. Men and women from all tribes strutted and showed off their Persian tunics and carpets. I, Tania, watched this preening and excitement with a strange sense of foreboding.

· · ·

THE AMAZONS STOPPED, awestruck, before a display of toys. Then, laughing and crying out in delight, they rushed at the trinkets, reaching out for them: figurines, puppets, automated animals worked by a system of leather straps, pretty ribbons, pouches filled with ravishing stones for board games, gold counters for flipping into the gaping mouths of carved frogs, abacuses with sleekly sliding beads, floating glass fish, imitation birds made with real feathers . . . in the middle of all this the man struggled to keep order, brandishing toys and waving his hands as he sputtered out his prices. His shouts amused and intimidated the girls, who backed away and stopped their laughing. They could not choose: taking did not come easily to us, we who had nothing.

I ventured over toward the spice trader to make my annual purchases. In a series of earthenware bowls blue, yellow, saffron, orange, purple, violet, and every shade of green mingled with a multitude of different whites. The price of spices had dropped that year: I sensed great changes. I followed my queen into the labyrinth of stalls displaying cloth. Fabrics fluttered over my face and stroked my hand. Rough, soft, fine, thick, transparent, opaque, sparkling, bleached, white, black, green, blue, orange, and red, all undulating in the wind and dancing in the sunlight. Dazzled, I looked away and kept my eyes on my feet: girls of Siberia could only afford the cheapest fabrics.

On the far side of a large tent we came across the pottery market with heaps of brightly colored vases, bowls, and plates decorated with geometric designs. The people of the steppes stood on their carpets, discussing prices and gesticulating with their hands. They used colored pebbles to keep their accounts and only exchanged goods on the last day of the market.

After pottery came the slave market, where near-naked men were exhibited with just a scrap of cloth over their hips. They lay in chains, playing dead. When anyone went near them they snapped open their eyes and watched with loathing, ready to pounce and bite.

The plant market was covered with a roof of fine cloth and provided cool shade and sumptuous perfumes. Exotic flowers with unpronounceable names stopped my queen in her tracks. She moved away and came back again. When she found a plant she liked, she stopped and looked at it so intently it might grow inside her head.

The sun was sinking and we headed back to our settlement still empty-handed but pleased with our walk. We did not allow ourselves anything luxurious, caring only for what was strictly necessary.

Many tents had been set up at the entrance to the market. Newly formed couples could spend the night in one at a price of three black pebbles. Crowds drifted to and fro, buying warm milk, alcohol, and grilled meats. Dogs barked, and goat kids tied to stakes bleated. From that tumult of different accents the language of the steppes reserved for negotiations emerged most clearly.

Men and women fell silent and parted to let the Amazon queen pass. Although small, she was radiant as the sun rising to announce a day of happy hard work. Her thick eyebrows, black eyes, and full lips all expressed her indomitable character. Following behind her, we confronted curious onlookers with our heads held high, clothed in our pride as if it were the most sumptuous of cloaks.

Despite her youth, our queen was respected and feared. Rather than tarnishing her beauty, slander conferred on her all the charm of legend. It was said that we were abductors of men, that we married them only to kill them the following day. It was said that the queen of the Amazons had magic in her belly to make a man invincible, and that was why so many warriors risked their lives to couple with her. Women in the crowds watched us warily, while the more daring men winked and smiled at us. Dusk was spreading; eyes sparkled, glances flitted like so many stars in the darkness, addressing us in a language that needed no words. Any Amazon drawn to one of these signals could leave us and throw herself onto whoever sent out the sign like an eagle swooping on its prey. She could take the man or woman who caught her eye and drag her catch off to a tent for a night's entertainment.

There was no exchange of gifts, nor of hair or blood. An ancestral statute dictated that we could not give a stranger anything that had once belonged to us. We had to leave as we arrived, in the swish of a gallop, with no oaths or promises. There were bound to be weaker girls among us who met up with the same lover—be it a man or a woman—once a year. In those tents they could make love and whisper to each other and weep. Back in our midst they had to hide their pain at being separated as if it were a shameful sickness. We permitted them to suffer in silence. With us they had to laugh even if they wanted to cry, to be strong and full of fight even if their hearts were torn apart.

Some girls disappeared during this annual gathering. We never pursued or punished those who left us. We considered this fall from grace to have been written in their stars. We barely even commented when a girl left: the moment she broke away from us, her name ceased to be heard, her face was erased from our memories. We considered that her soul had simply gone, just as it had once arrived in our midst. We, the daughters of the glacier, formed no attachments, not even to girls who had been our sisters.

The Amazons respected freedom; they were freedom. Anyone who chose suffering was free to live her suffering. None of us could stand in the way of fate. We knew nothing of punishment, we knew only our adoration of the God of Ice who watched over our earthly lives. The tribe's laws could be transgressed, for beyond laws, there was God.

· · ·

THE QUEEN WALKED on, face veiled and head held high, accompanied by clinking from the weapons fastened to her belt and by her twelve Amazons reputed to be bear-killers. Only innkeepers had the temerity to call out to her and compliment her. The queen replied to their greetings with a slight nod of her head. I sensed that she was suspicious, that she was looking for someone she was due to meet. She quickened her pace and went into a tent with a bouquet of white lilies over the door. She came straight back out again and gestured for us to leave.

That year the moon had just filled for the fourth time, and it was already summer. The daughters of Siberia were restless in the encampment; all around me I heard talk of a warrior from the land where the sun sets. The girls huddled around the fire wide-eyed and eager to tell the queen the rumors they had collected during the course of each day, all talking and exclaiming at the same time. They said he came from a coast peopled by fishermen who barely wore any clothes or finery. They said he had burned down cities and raped women. They said that with the treasures he had looted from Persian cities, he had bought mercenaries. They said that with his golden lance and on his great white horse he had dared challenge the Great King of Persia, and had declared he would take Babylon, the greatest city on earth.

The queen remained silent. I could tell she was preoccupied with some secret thought. I could read the sadness through her smiles. The night wore on, and the chattering girls grew quieter. Soon they fell silent, making way for the chirping of grasshoppers and the crackling of the fire. I lay not far from the queen and was woken by a slight sound. She lifted the tent door and went out; I followed her. She jumped onto her horse, I on mine. She left the encampment and headed for the very heart of the steppe. I kept a respectful distance without losing sight of her.

The moon poured an ocean of silvery light over the steppe. The Amazon queen stood by the banks of the river, a motionless silhouette, while time trickled by. The clouds scudded softly past, reflected in the water. They too were heading slowly for the horizon, never to return. Although I was far from her, I could sense her trembling. Was she cold? Was she afraid? Fierce warriors and famished tigers had not succeeded in shaking her. What was she waiting for? Had some nomad invited her to follow him? Was it a woman who had arranged to meet her here to join us as an Amazon? Since when had she grown so weak that she carried a secret in her heart? Talestria, my wild queen, the warrior with two weapons, how long had she been at war with herself?

All of a sudden I was aware of a man's singing above the rustling grass, at first indistinct and then loud and clear. The outline of a horseman etched itself against the moon as it sank toward the earth. Although I did not understand the words, I grasped their meaning: he was singing of love, its intoxicating pleasures and its pain.

Talestria shuddered. Why that shudder? Had they met the year before? Had they exchanged sweet nothings? Had they promised each other this night of love beside the river? Talestria, my queen, had she forgotten our battles with those men who loomed on the horizon, come to steal our sheep and massacre us? Had she forgotten those hostile horsemen and their obsessive desire to catch us and use our bellies to bring forth still more valiant warriors of the steppes? Talestria had schemed, lied, and cajoled to appease hostilities, to ensure their support and evade their traps. For our survival she had lowered her proud forehead before their powerful chiefs. She had led us into war when the peace fell apart. Why should my queen—who was impregnable to emotion or fear—be shaking so this evening?

Who was this man who could imitate the dawn chorus? Why did his voice carve through my heart and reduce me to tears? He rode toward Talestria with his stallion's head lowered in a submissive stance. The white feathers on his helmet quivered in the wind.

The stallion suddenly reared up, and the horseman swooped down on my queen, holding a stick armed with long spines in his hand. Talestria tugged at her mare's bridle, and the two horses brushed past each other. She held his stick firm with the spiked bludgeon in her left hand while, with one swift twist of the crescent-shaped blade in her right hand, she sliced off his head.

Talestria wiped her weapons and put them back into her belt. She set off without a backward glance. The horseman's torso slipped from his steed and slumped to the ground. Blood sprang from his gaping neck and formed a stream tenderly watering the steppe. Soon wolves drawn by the smell would come and tussle over the corpse. Then crows and scavengers would pick the skeleton clean. Flies would lick up the last vestiges of sun-dried blood. Talestria had been the faster. Talestria, queen of the Amazons, was a better warrior than any man who wanted her as his trophy. Such is the law of the steppes. The strong grow stronger once they have overcome weakness. The weak have to hide or perish.

The sun circled in the sky and the moon was growing more slender. We collected two newborn girls and exchanged a mare for three young slave girls. Once the little ones were strapped to our backs, we set off at a gallop for the ends of the earth.

"Never love an Amazon," children sang as they ran through the tall grass while their parents dismantled their tents and herded their sheep together. "They kill those who love them best . . ."

CHAPTER 3

Armed with lances, masked with leather blinkers and covered in armor, the horses charged. They collided, breast to breast, their legs clashing together; they reared up and trampled fallen soldiers. Their manes scattered showers of blood. The men's shouts mingled with the frantic whinnies of their mounts as they fell, never again to rise to their hooves. Arrows whistled through the air. Lances, shields, bludgeons, tridents, axes, and iron whips gleamed. Wherever a weapon flashed, blood sprang forth, organs spilled, limbs and heads fell. The smell of sweat, blood, and excrement was suffocating. I could no longer hear the drum roll. I could no longer make out the sun through the haze of white dust. I lost track of time. I was stepping into that eternity where men are reduced to incandescent patches, luminous halos. There was a hot liquid running over my face, a barbed whip had just ripped a piece of flesh from my thigh, an arrow had buried itself in my left side, the sharpened blade of a dagger had cut my arm to the bone. A heavy weapon struck me on the nape of the neck, and I staggered. That moment I knew my god had abandoned me. He had abandoned me to my own fate, to the Persian warriors who were still hurling themselves at me. I had to make the choice alone: to wake up or close my eyes, to let myself be carried off by the sweet torpor or to return to the horror and the shouting. Suddenly I could sense death breathing over me, hear its lascivious whispering. It wrapped me in its arms and rolled out a smooth calm road before me, stretching to the horizon. I don't want its monotonous peace! I don't want that bland gray, that platitude and inertia! Give me life in all its color and madness! Give me copulation and galloping horses and warfare! My body felt all its pain again. Strength returned, and with it the terrifying grimaces of the men around me, the froth on the horses' mouths. I brandished my sword. My standards followed its lead and advanced slowly but surely toward the east.

Darius, the Great King of Persia, had come to meet me, intending to crush me with an army of one hundred thousand men. His elephants and camels, his barbarian foot soldiers and armored cavalries, had filled the valleys and spread out across the plain. Confronted with this unprecedented deployment of troops, I opted for the strategy of exhaustion. The number three is perfection, while nine possesses the magic of infinity. I constrained Darius to a long duel of three cycles, each of which would be divided into three battles.

During the first cycle the enemy were more numerous, but Alexander's phalanxes were very disciplined. The Persians, who had believed they were invincible until then, were impressed by the temerity of my troops. The second cycle was a succession of badgering skirmishes. Trapped in its rigid formations, the Persian army was unable to defend itself from my cavalry's repeated surprise attacks. In the third cycle I ordered my battalions to lose. As soon as the Persians drew near, our soldiers had to throw down their arms and flee. To flatter Darius, I myself pretended to run in fear, leaving behind my golden helmet, which the Persians swiftly carried back to their king as a trophy.

The weather was magnificent on the day of the ninth engagement, but since dawn we could smell rain in the air. I reviewed my troops on horseback, riding a mount very like Bucephalus, who had succumbed to his wounds. No one had noticed the substitution. Everything around me had to contribute to the myth of an indestructible Alexander. I had manipulated certain elements to ensure that Apollo gave us a message of victory. On that decisive day I needed the complicity of this god, who was often silent in the face of my doubts and weaknesses.

Above the emaciated faces and wounded bodies of my troops I saw my standards floating in the wind. To the death, soldiers! Or to all the gold in the East! Life is so short; tomorrow, rubies and sapphires, velvet sheets and beautiful slave girls, will be ours! Let us take the spices and palaces and sumptuous feasts of conquerors! The arrows strike only cowards and spare the brave! The blood we lose makes us stronger; a severed arm, a gouged eye, only makes us all the more courageous! To battle, my men! If you die, you shall go home to rest; if you live, you shall sleep in Babylon!

From the top of the hill I watched the two armies throw themselves at each other like two great waves. My two look-alikes, each escorted by a commander's standard-bearer, fled in opposite directions. The Persian troops immediately followed them in the hopes of looting weapons, helmets, and saddles. Then, disguised as a lowly soldier, I rode down the hill with a cavalry detachment in light armor and sped to the rear of the Persian army, where Darius had his headquarters.

I confronted the showers of arrows with my eyes open. In our galloping frenzy, I grew taller, and death receded. Stupefied by the extraordinary phenomenon of a warrior who would not die, the barbarians believed I was the manifestation of a god. They threw down their arms and began to flee. Darius, the master of the Persian universe who had grown up in the suave luxury of oriental palaces surrounded by women and eunuchs, Darius, the demigod who had never wielded a weapon, was terrified by the war cries drawing closer to him. He lost any desire to fight and fled with his personal guard.

．　．　．

WITH THAT FLIGHT began his downfall.

The regent in Babylon, an ambitious eunuch, exploited the Great King's defeat, proclaiming himself master of the city and taking the royal children hostage. On hearing this, Darius decided not to return home and fled toward the mountains. Confusion reigned over his lands. Many towns surrendered, and many regiments capitulated without a fight. I learned that Darius was a weak man and had been manipulated by his eunuchs, who could think only of bickering for power and increasing their own wealth. Constantly traveling between the splendors and marvels of Babylon, Suse, and Persepolis, he had known nothing of the famines and epidemics in the provinces. As if deaf and blind, he had slowly released his authority at the expense of his governors, and so, thanks to him, the decadence that had ravaged the West reached the East.

Poor peasants, undernourished soldiers, and local dignitaries who had never been respected at court rushed after me and showered me with gifts. I was hailed everywhere as a liberator, as the one who had conquered the tyrant, I was encouraged to march on Babylon and drive out the usurper.

The regent tried to negotiate for peace by sending me finery, caravans filled with Darius's treasure. He promised me other fabulous riches if I continued to pursue Darius without stopping at the gates of his city. I sent him a herald with my reply: if he recognized Alexander as his master, he would be under my protection, shielded from challenges and insurrections.

Three days' march from Babylon I was greeted by a procession of royal dignitaries with incense and music. We signed a secret treaty: the regent would proclaim me master of Babylon, and I would entrust the running of the city to him.

On the horizon I could see the bronze gates piercing the very skies and stopping birds in flight. They opened before Alexander with the servile enthusiasm of a great courtesan spreading her legs for her richest client. Dressed as a lowly soldier, I watched with satisfaction as one of my look-alikes stepped into that ancient city crowned with golden laurels and dressed in my gold armor with scarlet straps. He was hoisted onto a cart and drawn triumphantly down the widest avenue in the world, waving proudly and indulgently to the prostrations of the Chaldeans and Persians.

The wind blew, and the hanging gardens scattered a shower of petals.

. . .

THE TOWER OF Babel had disappeared; Babylon had become that Tower of Babel, carrying off its inhabitants, its palaces and gardens, its streets and canals, in a giant spiral toward the heavens. Wide avenues wound round networks of sinuous little streets. To make the streets more passable the Babylonians uprooted trees and bushes, replanting them on roofs and terraces high up on pillars. But still carts, traps, camels, and horses jostled for space. The streets became blocked and then cleared for no apparent reason. Shops, restaurants, smoke houses, taverns, and baths kept their doors open day and night. The crowds drifted in and out; they went up steps into high-perched houses decorated with balustrades, or down underground where snatches of incantatory music wafted from dark rooms lined with cushions and lit by lanterns. The rustle of clothing and clacking of shoes mingled with clinking glasses, the clip-clop of horses' hooves, the hubbub of conversation, and the bustle of waking households. The high, painted city walls resonated with the echoes of all this never-ending life, emitting a muffled buzz that grew louder with every new dawn.

Temples dedicated to the gods occupied street corners: people from all over the world, dressed in every kind of costume, went there to pray in every language. Each wore the perfume of his or her country. Every variety of incense from every land blended with every smell of every different style of cooking. Newborns were greeted according to a thousand different customs, and the dead were left naked or shrouded, burned or mummified, buried or left to scavengers. Each individual went to heaven or to the shades on horseback or by boat, in chains or on beating wings.

The roar and bustle of the greatest metropolis on earth stopped at the foot of the City of the King. This town within a town was crammed with administrators' palaces and ministers' residences. Built with blocks of beaten earth and painted inside and out, they shamelessly displayed their splendor. As the sun set, an entire population of plants and animals came to life as if trying to break away from those facades: monkeys squabbled along the walls; parrots called from the rooftops; dogs ran alongside leopards; bees plundered roses and carnations. A bird with the head of a vulture and a long shining tail had pride of place on the pediments. I learned that it was called the phoenix. Every hundred thousand years it died in flames and was reborn from the ashes.

What secret shame I felt as I cast my eye over the conquerors and the conquered! On the one side, Macedonians and Greeks, their heads bare, their linen tunics leaving their arms, shoulders and legs for all to see, their leather sandals revealing hairy feet and filthy black toenails. On the other, Persian administrators in turbans, wearing rich brocade all the way down to their shoes which were embroidered with gold. They each held a different flower in their hands as a symbol of their responsibilities. They were followed by eunuchs, imperial slaves with shaven heads, who wore vests over their short tunics and ballooning pants threaded with gold. An evolved civilization clothes its people; it covers their flesh, ties their hair, and decks out their limbs with precious stones to distinguish them from animals. I who had conquered

Darius must have looked to the Persians like the leader of a band of savages set loose in the Orient.

In Pella life had only five colors: green like the fields, yellow like wood, white like houses, blue like the sea, and black like the earth. When the regent opened the gates to the citadel of pleasure, I was accosted by a profusion of unfamiliar colors carried on a blend of subtle perfumes.

The eunuch who had sold Babylon to Alexander smiled and bowed. He walked backward before me and called for a bevy of castrated young musicians to sing the praises of my victory. His head was bare, and he wore a heavy amber necklace. His triple chin quivered, and his eyes—one tawny and one blue—studied me surreptitiously. He was holding a bracelet, nervously rolling the ruby and emerald beads in his fat fingers. He led me straight to the bedchamber of his former master, offering me his bed, his slaves, and his gynaeceum.

· · ·

IN THE HEART of the city of Babylon was the City of the King. In the heart of the City of the King was the City of Pleasure. At its highest point, up in the heavens, was my bedchamber.

The warriors' screams and the clash of arms ceased to haunt my ears. I heard only birdsong and the sibilant murmur of fountains. The most beautiful garden in the world stretched out beneath my arched windows, wiping away sorrows of the past and concerns for the future. The Euphrates snaked through meadows dotted with roses, violets, and carnations, and edged with orange trees and jasmine, and it spilled its ripples peacefully into ponds covered with water lilies.

I lay on the bed and forgot the incandescent sun, the cruel wind, the endless marching. I swam in a sea of cushions, heaped around me, soft and giving. A curtain the size of a tent was draped over my bed, and through it I glimpsed the cupola-shaped ceiling—a clear demonstration of the Persians' superiority in science and architecture. There were no pillars or support beams in that vast room: the substantial roof was held up by the six walls thanks to an ingenious distribution of its weight, calculated in a way the Greeks had not mastered. The frescoes were lit by candelabras that never went out. At the tops of the walls flowers blossomed between geometrical patterns. At eye level there were panels covered with a fine layer of gold, and Darius himself was represented as a handsome young man in his royal turban. A sequence of scenes from his daily life were depicted: reading, reciting poetry, chasing butterflies, watching monkeys dance, riding on an elephant, picnicking, bathing . . . and even in his bath the fallen king wore his turban. Loving embraces followed on from languorous walks, and poems in calligraphy accompanied the images. Beneath the panels were mosaics depicting a limpid spring edged with exotic vegetation. Among the countless faces of his beautiful and sensual young concubines, I noticed a favorite—small with very white skin and huge eyes over a small mouth—who featured in all the scenes of pleasure.

Hephaestion came to greet me, telling me Cassander was angered by these frescoes to Darius's glory, and wanted to replace them with scenes of Alexander's battles. I cast my eyes over Darius's chests of different perfumes, his musical instruments, his carpets of spun gold . . . and I started to laugh.

I, Alexander, son of Olympias, whore of Philip, usurper of

the League of Corinth, had become master of Babylon. It was a miracle I could barely believe.

The scars on my body counted out the battles won with force and fury. The calluses on my hands told of enemies defeated and lands conquered. Nothing else about me or on me proved that I was master of Macedonia, Greece, Egypt, Arabia, and Persia. I felt as if I had cheated: that was why I laughed. Since the dawn of time the earthly crown had been waiting for just one master. All those who longed for it had failed. I had grasped it, but not because I had greater strength, better tactics, or more determination. I, Alexander of Macedonia, was not afraid of the stars of decadence. Where other men retreated, I advanced. Where other men gave up, I persevered.

. . .

HEPHAESTION, MY FRIEND, why do Darius's courtiers speak Greek when none of our generals speak Persian?

Why do Cassander, Perdiccas, and Crateros insist on wearing worn old sandals when Darius's slaves wear embroidered shoes?

Why did the West close its doors on the East, claiming it was barbarian?

I, Alexander, shall wear oriental dress and learn the language of the defeated. I want the East and the West to unite, the luxuries of Persia to combine with our philosophy, the strength of Macedonia to flourish in the beauty of oriental art. I want our bloods to mix. I shall send Persian women to the Greek islands so their children can benefit from two languages and a double inheritance. I shall drive away the bandits who prowl the trading routes and put the corrupt Persian army back on a sound footing.

Tradesmen will no longer be subject to extortion: from now on our soldiers will protect their caravans. Alexander will open up the free market between East and West.

Hephaestion, do you understand what the forced marches were for, wearing down soldiers' feet and torturing their legs? Do you understand why horses died and soldiers starved and the incandescent sun blinded us and drove men mad? Do you understand the reason for the murders, executions, and massacres? A far greater good can emerge from evil!

Without violence there would be no exchange. Without the war led by Alexander, all these peoples—the Greeks, the Macedonians, the Persians, the Chaldeans, the Jews, the Egyptians, and the Arabs—would never have agreed to embrace each other.

Don't you see, it is here, in Babylon, in Darius's bed, that my fate has been revealed. I have conquered peoples, and those peoples have conquered me. For them I shall design a new civilization, a new world, that of the phoenix rising from the ashes.

The eunuch who has already betrayed one master must die of a sudden fever. I shall confer the regency of Babylon on Mazee, Darius's general who fought valiantly against Alexander.

Crateros shall be the arm mercilessly brandishing my sword. One by one, Darius's sons—both legitimate and illegitimate—shall be tracked down and decapitated. You, Hephaestion, who love medicine, you must learn Persian remedies and magic. You shall heal my wounds and give succor to my soul.

•　•　•

THE DOOR OF the imperial gynaeceum opened to reveal thousands of women's bodies, offerings given by the empire's twenty satrapies. Princesses, noblewomen, daughters of the common people, daughters of vassal tribes, girls captured by nomadic cavalries . . . all had been Darius's slaves, captive to his desires.

Young, old, barely out of childhood, blond, brunette, white, black, women from every land on earth were represented here, living imprisoned in a vast room covered in carpets and decorated with pools and fountains. They slept, urinated, danced, embraced, sang, and ate in a hubbub of moans, cries, sighs, and laughter, all indifferent to onlookers or to the smell of putrefaction and excrement. Eunuchs circulated among them, some serving, others cracking a whip. I was informed that since Darius fled, the attendants in the City of Pleasure had stopped cleaning the gynaeceum and only fed the women once a day. Their eyes looked dull and empty for lack of air and freedom, like birds with clipped wings no longer dreaming of the sky. In all that dying flesh I found the king's favorite, the one painted on all the walls of his bedchamber. She was lying naked on a carpet, sobbing and weeping, her hair disheveled. Her body was covered with scars and scabs. I learned that after Darius's defeat the other women had scratched and bitten and trampled on her.

I gave orders for these women to be released, and handed each of them enough money to travel home. I myself washed and fed Jasmine, the woman whom the Great King had loved, and led her to my room. Although quite lucid now, she would not say anything. She was happy simply taking refuge in my arms. In my absence she stayed on the bed, motionless, occasionally sweeping her cold, joyless eyes over the frescoes depicting moments of happiness she no longer recognized. She had turned my room into another prison.

When I finally decided to give her freedom, she claimed she

knew where her parents lived. She refused an escort, took the money I gave her, and left.

They say Jasmine drifted about the city. They say she went mad all over again. Babylonians, if on your travels through these sinuous streets you chance across a little girl with disheveled hair, walking barefoot and singing and muttering to herself, give her water, give her bread, do not throw stones at her! It is Jasmine, once cherished by Darius, the most powerful of kings, tended for a while by Alexander, the most intrepid warrior. Babylonians, step aside and let this girl pass, this girl who harbors the secret of her loves in her breast.

. . .

GIANT SAILING SHIPS unfurled their sails and plied up and down the Euphrates. Smaller boats laden with goods, like fish teeming round marine monsters, tossed and jostled in their wake. Persia was the country of excess.

Every quarter of the city had its own libraries, vast palaces with rooms in which the erudite from all lands could come to eat, sleep, and work. A royal annuity allowed them to lead an intellectual life with no concern for the contingencies of their day-to-day existence. This decree attracted the wise from all over the world, and the Achemenides opened the gates of the City of the King to all, offering them positions in their countless ministries. Compared to the number of Persian officials, the Ecclesia in Athens and the Macedonian council were mere child's play, but the Persians had the intelligence to simplify complexity.

The Great Kings made no decisions without consulting the academies of arithmetics and of astrologers.

The Academy of Manners oversaw good relations between different peoples.

The Academy of Architects designed towns and palaces.

The Academy of Sports organized horse races.

The Academy of Agriculture sent its inspectors and specialists to the very limits of the empire.

The Academy of Water was responsible for wells, irrigation, and waterborne trade.

The Academy of Industry built roads and dams.

There were academies of painting, perfumes, lamps, ceramics, slave management, weaving, royal animals, and medicine, each gathering, classifying, devising, and making official its respective specialty.

The Academy of Poets was associated exclusively with royal life. Poets followed the king and, in beautiful calligraphy, had to write poems inspired by every situation: audiences, receptions, banquets, journeys. When men are long gone . . . poetry remains. It transforms everyday moments into historical fragments. The Great Kings of Persia knew how to make themselves immortal.

The Academy of Music inventoried fashionable tunes and composed official melodies. Wherever the king went, he heard music appropriate to the place and his activities.

Poetry and music are man's most beautiful adornments.

. . .

THE CENTER OF Babylon was occupied by dignitaries and the rich; the poor lived around the outskirts of the city, in low-slung houses made of wood and beaten earth. They all had favorite taverns, be they luxurious or tumbledown, where men could meet and talk.

They drank infusions of leaves from the lands around the Indus, and they circulated a long pipe connected to a flask of water.

"Beyond Persian territories lie the lands of the Indus," announced the head of the Order of Merchants, who had invited me into a sumptuous tavern reserved for his personal use.

The merchants were not common stall keepers, I gathered from Mazee, Darius's former general who had become my most fervent servant. Throughout Persian lands, merchants were respected and stall keepers despised. The Persians considered that merchants transported the wonders of this world from one country to another, while stall keepers robbed their own neighbors in the market square.

I drank the infusion and pretended to enjoy his pipe. The smoke made me nauseous, and my head spun, but I decided to please Oibares, the most influential man in Babylon.

In this empire so avid for wealth and exoticism, merchants governed from behind the scenes, and extended their invisible power to the very limits of the earth. The richest of them owned as many as ten caravans, which came and went in rotation to ensure a constant stream of new goods. Supplying kings and satraps, selling weapons and working as spies, with an intimate knowledge of distant inaccessible lands, they knew how to manipulate tribal chiefs and corrupt armies. They brought messages of peace or delivered declarations of war. In order to protect their own best interests, they were affiliated with the Order of Merchants, which controlled the trading routes, set out the laws, and settled disagreements. Every ten lunar years the merchants held a great nocturnal ceremony during which they threw straws into a vase to elect a new leader.

Oibares was forty-five, with shining blue eyes, a fine proud nose, and thin lips. Like all rich Babylonians obsessed with their appearance, he wore a scarlet turban on his shaven head, and had a long beard in which his own hair was blended with extensions. He created magnificent arrangements with it, dying it chestnut brown, curling it with hot irons, and perfuming it with rosewater. Disappointed with such a weak, extravagant king, Oibares had plotted against Darius, who constantly raised taxes and closed his eyes when his troops plagued trading caravans.

The elegance of Oibares' appearance was a perfect camouflage for his thoughts. As it was impossible to guess what his intentions were, I disarmed him with my submissive-woman behavior. I let him talk without interrupting: encouraged by my complicit silence, intoxicated by my loving gaze, he took long drags on his pipe and exhaled lightheartedly. The smoke scrolled around us like drunken bacchantes dancing languidly to the rhythm of his voice.

"Have you heard tell, Great Alexander, of the lands of the Indus, lands of deepest valleys and darkest forests?" he asked. "The men who live there are wild and cruel. Their swamps are full of slithering snakes and birds that spit fetid venom. No one has conquered those kingdoms since time immemorial. But you, Alexander of Macedonia, son of Apollo, invincible warrior who was granted Ammon's benediction, you shall conquer the nine-headed monsters with tiger's teeth and serpent's tails. You, the man whom all the gods love, shall take the treasure defended by those tribes of men and apes."

Oibares clapped his hands, and a slave appeared, carrying a tray of raw gold, rubies, sapphires, emeralds, and pearls. He put the tray down on a low table and left us. Oibares picked up a piece of emerald, rubbed it on his sleeve, and looked at it. He gave a sigh.

"*Oha*, Great Alexander, master of Babylon and Memphis! You alone deserve all the jewels of the Orient! Do you know that in the days when the earth was covered with snow and frost, there was an ocean where the Indus is now, in the land where the sun rises? There were dragons, huge aquatic snakes covered in scales, living in the eternal darkness of those abyssal depths. Every three moons they uncoiled their monstrous heavy bodies and came to the surface to wait for dawn. When the sun rose, they squirmed and writhed together, throwing themselves out of the water to draw in the light, their celestial sustenance. But time passed, and the land emerged from the depths. The dragons died, and their gigantic bodies turned into mines of precious stones in which the incandescent sun still burned. The seed borne by the females became a seam of diamonds holding the vital force of that long-gone world in its very heart."

Oibares stroked his beard, his eyes lost in thought, as if gazing at that distant land so dangerous it gave its riches a sensual glamour. All of a sudden he flipped the tray over with a disdainful swipe of his hand. The precious stones scattered and rolled across the carpet.

"The stones of the twenty satrapies of Persia are but pebbles! In the land of the Indus the gold is heavy and the gems dazzling! *Oha*, Great Alexander, the only man destined to be Master of Asia, the only king worthy of ascending to the throne in the heart of the sun, the only hero who will make a vast crown of glory from the treasures of the earth, I shall give you whatever gold you need to raise the greatest army in the world! In exchange for this humble service, you shall carve a route for us, we who transport the colors and savors of life, a route from here right to the sun!"

I found Oibares pleasing: his poetry, his fiery admiration for unknown lands, his passion for life, lent a certain grandeur to his mercenary calculations. I liked his intelligent mind, which had spotted an ally in me. I particularly appreciated the finesse with which he manipulated, offering and submitting before receiving or asking. He had just suggested a deal that would join his interests to my ambitions. Carried forward by Persian soldiers and supported by merchants, I could conquer the entire world.

I lay down my pipe and took off my rings, mounted with the most beautiful stones from the lands I had conquered; then I threw them in the air like trifles. They rolled over toward the Persian pebbles.

"Glaciers are melting, seas are drying out, dragons are turning into diamonds, and one day they will be dust. Worldly riches come and go. Alexander wants celestial riches, the ocean of gold pieces that belongs to whoever reaches the summit! In that place where Alexander is heading the earth trembles, citadels burn down, city walls are breached, roads appear. Alexander builds and destroys fortunes. Those who follow him ride with him toward all that is vast and magnificent."

Oibares looked me in the eye and then burst out laughing. Contaminated by this rush of exuberance, I laughed with him and concluded our unprecedented alliance between East and West, between the power of gold and the strength of the lance.

· · ·

THE MERCHANTS BUSIED themselves putting together an army for me. To secure absolute loyalty toward me from Darius's former soldiers, they opened up the succession of heavy bronze doors leading to the fortified chamber suspended between the sky and the earth, where the princess, the hidden pearl, the daughter and granddaughter of Great Kings, was waiting for her liberator.

Her perfume reached me before she appeared; and the rustle of her tunic already filled the room in which I sat. Preceded by two eunuchs and followed by two governesses, she approached with all the confidence and majesty of an imperial daughter. She was tall and slender, with white skin. Her brown hair had been coiled around hot irons and now fell in floating curls about her heavily jeweled headdress. She gave a slight bow and knelt before me. With lowered eyes she waited for me to hold out my hand to her, thereby sealing the union between Persians and Macedonians.

Olympias would have been furious to see me wed a barbarian. Behind the princess Hephaestion, Cassander, and Perdiccas stood like statues, frozen in icy pride, their faces betraying vehement indignation. City dignitaries nervously fluttered their peacock-feather fans, determined to see the end of the Achemenides dynasty. There was palpable impatience in these Babylonians already dreaming of a newborn leader, a legitimate master of both East and West, their future emperor, he who would make Babylon the center of the world.

Mazee, the new regent, gave me a wink, a signal urging me to reach out my hand as a symbol of my acceptance. But this girl of royal blood was a disappointment to me! Kneeling humbly at my feet, she proved to be an insignificant creature, without music or color, a vessel, a simple recipient for the male seed, ready to conceive and give birth. I felt no emotion. The infantile excitement of seeing my dream realized had just come crashing down. She was not the young woman in red waiting for me at the top of a rock. My precious pearl was not here.

Instead of holding out my hand to her, I stiffened and announced:

"Princess, I grant you my protection. You, your mother, and your sisters may keep your titles and privileges from the previous reign. You need be afraid of nothing from now on. May you be venerated like members of my own family!"

Cassander was moved to cough, Hephaestion smiled, Perdiccas wiped his brow. The Babylonians, disconcerted, withdrew, and the princess followed their lead, returning to her gilded prison. I spent a feverish night, tossing and turning in the vast imperial bed, wondering whether I was condemned to be a king without a queen, a conqueror without an heir. Was this the sacrifice expected of a man spoiled by the gods?

The following morning Oibares asked to speak with me. Unable to insist I take a particular wife, he made me a second and final proposition: to convert me to their religion so that the supreme god, the source of all light and creator of the world, Ahura Mazda, might invest me as the only king over many and the only master of many. A brief presentation of the religion founded by Zarathustra was all I needed. Ahura Mazda, the all-powerful winged god, reminded me of the Demiurge venerated by Aristotle. Without losing any more time, I arranged the ceremony for the following day and dismissed Oibares, still reeling from the speed of my decision.

The incantations grew louder as I stepped into the dark interior of a massive temple, its long aisle lined with fires. The ceremony had to be interrupted for an awkward incident: the magi wanted to shave the middle of my head and make me wear a turban—a barbarian practice that I refused. The procession was suspended, and the debate lasted three days, dividing all of Persia. The future of the empire was saved when one magus found a passage in an ancient text citing a king who had been converted without having his head shaved. Reciting prayers all the while, the priests threw me into a pool and purified me. They dressed me in a scarlet tunic and allowed me to wear a wreath of golden laurels, the crown conferred on me by the Macedonians and Greeks.

The magi consecrated me and gave me the name Akassam, the warrior of fire. They revealed to me a very ancient prediction that foretold the arrival of a warrior from the West. Dressed in red and gold, he would bear the fire of the winged gods all the way to the Far East. Every soldier who followed him and took part in that sacred war would be handsomely rewarded after death. They would live happily in celestial houses, surrounded by women and children.

That evening, in my dreams, I was back on the battlefield. Arrows whistled by; lances flew. I felt the hunger and thirst of combat. The soft cushions, indolent eunuchs, and intoxicating flattery were beginning to soften my mind and relax my muscles. Thirty days had been for Alexander what three years would be for an ordinary man. My time was counted. My life belonged to forced gallops, to the wind, and to unknown lands.

A woman was waiting for me, in a distant land, at the very top of a steep, rugged rock.

CHAPTER 4

The kings and queens of other countries wore crowns and held scepters. The chiefs and their wives in other tribes lived in tents embroidered with gold thread, ate from silver plates, and wore shimmering tunics. Talestria, queen of the Amazons, had no jewels or sumptuous gowns. She was not crowned. She simply dazzled. She was queen and warrior chief by her wisdom and strength.

Talestria held no scepter. She had no powers. No one in our tribe liked power. The word was forbidden, cursed. To us, the daughters of the steppe, women who valued freedom, our queen was like the nectar hidden in the heart of a flower. She was that fragrance transmitted from generation to generation.

The spirits of our ancestors chose one girl as the incarnation of their power. The queen was our voice to communicate with the invisible world. She was the path that led us to the Siberian glacier.

I, Tania, did not know where my queen had been born. All the girls in our tribe had been abandoned as children. What did her mother and father matter, what did it matter which blood flowed in her veins? Talestria was betrothed to the God of Ice. She was the daughter of autumn and winter. She conversed with horses, sang with the birds, and read the stars. She held the secret of the spirits in the palm of her hand. She reigned over the seasons, over time as it sped past and fled, over eternity.

In the kingdom of the girls who love horses the sky was our timepiece and the trees our calendar. That is why the ancestors dictated that, wherever we went, we should plant trees for the girls who would pass there hundreds of moons later. They would cut their trunks and read the years that lay between us and them by the rings traced in the wood. Trees were an invisible river allowing us to go back in time or navigate the future.

Once a year we celebrated the queen's birthday, even though not one of us knew the date of her birth. Our ancestors decreed that the day of the previous queen's death marked the birth of the new queen. During that year's celebrations Talestria was sixteen.

She was decked in flowers, and her loose hair floated in the wind. She stood in the middle of a clearing, and we, the daughters of the steppe, danced around her. We threw flowers at her, and leaves and catkins. She smiled and accepted our homage without a word. Then we scattered in the long grass, where a great banquet had been prepared over several days. We ate, drank, sang, danced, and laughed. At nightfall we gathered around a huge fire. The eldest of our number narrated legends she had learned from those who were no longer. We fell asleep one by one beneath the starry sky.

We woke at dawn to the whinnying of horses. A new year was beginning for us, and with it came the great gallop to the market of the steppes.

. . .

IN THE MARKET there were new faces: men in luxurious clothes selling off their jewels, and soldiers bartering over looted spoils. All around us people were talking in Persian, and this made me wary. This empire, which cultivated its taste for power, had been casting its covetous eye over the vast steppes for some time. Its military intrusions had been valiantly rebuffed by warriors from all the tribes working in unison. During our frenetic headlong gallops we sometimes crossed into its territory. From the rocky mountaintops we would watch caravans passing far below. Laden with worldly goods like ants toiling with pieces of food ten times their own size, they crawled laboriously over the arid land. The Persian Empire is the kingdom of men. We, the daughters of the steppe, are the birds of the glacier.

I lost no time finding the explanation for this pandemonium, and hurried to explain it to the queen. Alexander, the warrior who came from the West with his army of lancers and crossbow-men, had defeated Darius, the Great King of Persia. Babylon had fallen, and part of the Persian army had joined the ranks of the invading foreigner, setting off in pursuit of Darius, who had fled eastward. Alexander's name was on everyone's lips in every language. People said he was intelligent and beautiful as no man had ever been. They said that, decked in armor that flashed golden rays of light up to the very clouds, he had launched himself at the ramparts at the head of his army, and that no arrow could harm him. They also said this king liked only men; he was not drawn to a woman's flesh, had rejected Darius's three thousand concubines in Babylon, and declined the princess's proposal of marriage. They said he did not want to be the Great King of Persia, he wanted to be master of the world.

Talestria smiled. I asked why she was not worried like the chiefs of other tribes.

"Why worry?" she asked me.

"None of this bodes well. A powerful king has defeated an emperor. The Persian Empire that acted as our shield has fallen. The West will reach farther and farther into the East."

"Tania, we can wield weapons as well as any man. If the enemy appear on our horizon tomorrow, we shall fight them."

"Alexander, the son of a warrior and a sorceress, wants to be master of the world. His appetite knows no limits. He tortures and kills anyone who resists him. His army rapes the women in its path. Not satisfied with invading lands, they sow their seed and multiply using the wombs of the defeated. With such a strategy they will turn every free people into slaves!"

"The world is in decline," said Talestria. "The Persians were weakened by their wealth. Babylon was conquered because it had walls instead of wings. We, the daughters of Siberia, form attachments to nothing; we have no houses, no land, no fields, no gardens. We are invisible and invincible. We shall defend our freedom down to the last of our number. Death is nothing, you know that."

There was great agitation among the one hundred tribes of the steppes. Concerned about Darius's defeat and Alexander's advances, the chiefs wanted to find a common strategy to bar the way for the West. Some advocated a temporary tactical sub-mission, citing those cities that had resisted and then perished in flames. Others sang the praises of courage and combat. Others suggested the possibility of sending men to infiltrate Alexander's army, to secure his trust and then put mortal poison in his food. Still others put forward the idea of a counterattack: We should invade Persia, they said.

The discussions went on for ten days. The debates were punc-tuated with banquets, when the men succumbed to alcohol, and sang and danced. The queen and I stood in our corner, watching impassively.

As usual, the kings reached no agreement, each afraid the others would steal his cattle while he was at war with Alexander. The men of the steppes had many, many discussions but never made any decisions. Tempers flared; they argued and then dis-persed like a swarm of flies.

The tribes withdrew with their men, women, children, and flocks. Talestria, queen of the Amazons, ordered us to sharpen our weapons and stay vigilant on our homeward journey. She had spotted numerous Persian spies mingling in the Great As-sembly. In her thoughts she had heard the inner murmurings of the tribal chiefs. These cunning ambitious men had decided to profit from the atmosphere of fear: they planned to devour the weaker tribes.

• • •

THE WIND MADE the white clouds billow. Green waves of veg-etation reared up and crashed down toward us, then flattened to let us pass. A girl who had been sent ahead as a scout returned announcing that there were hundreds of horsemen in the hills. Talestria ordered us to slow our pace and form a line of attack.

A square formation of soldiers appeared, wearing magnificent clothes dulled by the dust. Their purebred horses looked exhausted; I had never seen such beautiful stallions, so tall and fine with long, thick manes. Ten men came forward from the ranks till they were one arrow's range from us. They called out to tell us that the Great King of Persia wanted to speak with our queen.

A quiver ran through the troops, and the soldiers stood aside as one man rode along the alley formed by the imperial guard. He had a long curly beard and wore a white coat muddied by wind and rain, and a white turban dripping with jewels. Talestria urged on her chestnut horse and went to meet him.

"By the power of He who holds the Mysteries of Creation and governs life from the highest spheres of heaven," cried the man, "I, Darius, king of the eternal fire, ask to speak with the queen of the Amazons."

"I am queen of the warriors of Siberia, of the white birds with red heads and of winged horses," Talestria replied in Persian. "Why, King Darius, have you ventured all the way to the steppes?"

"I have waited three days and three nights for you, *oha*, mistress of arrow-throwers, queen of soothsayers. I came to you because the world is at war, because the world is in flames. Only the magic ice of Siberia can put out the venomous flame of the setting sun."

"We, the daughters of freedom and speed, we cast aside evil spirits in the wake of our mares with their flaming red manes. We are not a mercenary army. We lend our strength only to the will of our God. If you follow the path of the stars for ten days' gallop from here, you will find the powerful warmongering kings of the Scythians. They will forget the rancor of the past and provide you with an army of archers."

"The kings of the Scythians do not know the secret of the glacier. Their fierce warriors were defeated by your weapons forged by the People of the Volcano. No one on earth has the power to make a man invincible. We, the men clothed in white light, we, the spirits with folded wings, we throw ourselves at your feet, *oha*, divine priestess of a vanished world. Your people and mine are branches of the same tree."

"We," replied Talestria, "the daughters of the ice, the indomitable birds who sing of our ancestors' pride, shall give your soldiers food and drink. We shall tend to your injured and to your horses. But you must set out again tomorrow morning when the sun returns to the steppe. Come, Darius, I offer you my tent and my hospitality tonight."

Darius and my queen dismounted, and on this signal, the two armies set up camp at the foot of the hill. The girls handed round remedies and shared out food among the Persian soldiers. Their colored eyes and curly beards were a source of great curiosity. The girls hovered around them cautiously like little birds not wanting to frighten away their prey. Suddenly, one of them grabbed hold of a beard, and the other pulled the man's hair. When the soldier cried out in pain, the girls ran away, unable to stifle their laughter.

The conversation between Talestria and Darius continued after the meal inside the queen's tent. Two scribes were called for—myself, Tania, who kept a wary eye on the defeated king, and a young Persian with no beard or turban.

Now clean and with his beard combed, Darius had put on a shimmering tunic and a less imposing turban. His exquisite perfume hung in the air. His hands rested on his knees, glittering—he had a jewel on every finger. I loathed his fine features, his haughty expression and slow, graceful movements. Flames from the animal-fat candles danced in the shadows. Talestria sat at the far end of the carpet from him. Although small, she somehow looked imposing. Without jewels and wearing a scarlet robe, she dominated the Great King with the sheer strength of her expression.

Without any further preliminaries, Darius proposed sharing his empire with my queen. My hand holding the reed trembled, and I looked up. That long face with blue lines around the eyes hid an impenetrable heart. Why was he offering his empire to a queen who owned nothing?

On the steppes women liked to speak ill of us, and men, though they cursed us, dreamed of capturing us and forcing us to bear their seed. Our queen was inaccessible and elusive; people compared her to a venomous flower that killed all those who wanted to pick it. Why was this man, Darius, Great King of Persia, apparently not afraid of my queen?

Darius spread a vast display of jewels before Talestria. He said he had another ten chests of precious stones of the same quality, and was prepared to offer them to the queen if she would become his wife. He said that in his kingdom they had dug into the heart of a mountain to create a stronghold housing millions of chests of precious items bequeathed by his ancestors, and that this mountain of treasures would bear the name Talestria if the queen agreed to join him. He told her that his empire had ten million horses, each more beautiful and more swift than the last.

He claimed he was master of a million white elephants, of a billion bees and birds, master of millions of men and women. If Talestria married him, he said, she would be mistress of the most extensive kingdom on earth. She would have a life of pleasure, dress in beautiful fabrics, and be served by the loveliest women. Agile acrobats would make her laugh, the very flowers would bow when she walked by; the whole universe would sing to the glory of Talestria, the mother of a new dynasty.

Darius became impassioned, reciting a poem he had just composed for Talestria:

Be praised, mother of myths.
Be praised, she who shall bear new divinities.
Your lineage shall venerate you for ten thousand years.
Your people shall give you oblations for one hundred thousand
  years.
Oha, divine mother of thunder and lightning,
Glorious souls await at your gates,
Waiting to be conceived and brought into this world.
They promise you the most beautiful crown known to men:
Seven branches of gold and nine diamonds,
Eighteen rubies and twenty-four emeralds,
Thirty-six sapphires and eighty pearls,
Twenty-five amethysts, eight onyx,
Five continents and eight oceans.

Bearing children, that was Talestria's magic power to change fate, to turn the tide of time! That was Darius's immortality, the advent of his power! It was said that Alexander had killed all

Darius's heirs. That was why the defeated king had come to ask Talestria to be the womb and the wet nurse of his descendants.

He edged closer to my queen on his knees and said:

"Talestria, be my queen tonight. Your warrior-women will protect and raise my heirs. You will rally the peoples of the steppes and expand the Persian Empire. I, Darius, must do my honor's bidding: I must go back to war. My God tells me I must avenge myself and die. But my children, forged by the eternal fire and blessed by the glacier of Siberia, will be invincible. Darius will have lost an empire, but his blood will flow in the veins of his children. Although conquered, he will be master of the world for all eternity."

A great cooing of promises, praises, and declarations of love fell from Darius's lips. My queen let him speak and said not a word. She smiled. From time to time I saw her eyes twinkle. I was worried. Was she seduced by this liar who was in love with power and wealth? Talestria must not betray the oath she had made to our God that she would never form an attachment with a man. She could not have a child!

The night wore on. Darius's eloquence frayed and tired. Talestria remained upright, motionless, and still she gave no answer. Dawn broke over the tent, and the birds' shadows could already be seen moving. The Persian scribe was asleep. Darius, exhausted and in despair, blinked his eyes to keep them open.

Suddenly the queen spoke:

"Darius, your destiny as king is at an end. The God of Ice is putting you to the test. You must climb the glacier without adornment, without a horse, without a royal turban. At its summit you will find a priceless treasure."

Darius's face lit up.

"To please you, I shall go in pursuit of it."

Talestria smiled.

"This treasure is in your heart, but the road there has been barred. Try to find your way instead of making war. Life or death, you can still choose."

After a brief silence she gave an enigmatic smile and added: "Dying is living."

Darius thought for a moment. I, Tania, had noted all this down without understanding it. My queen rose to her feet, arranged her crumpled tunic, and left the tent, and I followed behind.

We set off again toward the land of the white cranes with the crimson heads.

CHAPTER 5

Reinforcements came from Greece, and my Macedonian lieutenants put them in training with the Persian soldiers. I gathered information on the eastern territories and drew up better maps of them. At the head of a new army subjected to Macedonian discipline and reinforced with the battalions of camels and elephants abandoned by Darius, I marched toward eastern Persia.

Suse capitulated without a fight, but a riot erupted inside the city. The leader, a slave who had been driven out of the palace by the eunuchs after Darius's downfall, and who claimed he was the son of the winged god, had incited the poor to rebel. The uprising was swiftly quashed, and Bagoas chained and thrown at my feet. He was a slender young Persian with black hair and green eyes. The hatred, insolence, and religious fervor in those eyes bore right through me.

With that first glance from him, I forgot the order to have him executed and his body displayed for all to see. Kneeling at the foot of the dais, he seemed to know no fear, staring me down and making me uncomfortable. I, Alexander, master of the world, flushed as I ordered that he should be thrown into a dungeon. But I was haunted by his face, I could not sleep, and longed to hold him in my arms, to bring him suffering and pleasure.

I called for Hephaestion the very next morning and talked of my many concerns before tackling the question itself: I told him I would pardon the beautiful Bagoas, leader of the rioters, but that he would be punished with castration and would become my servant. Hephaestion smiled bitterly, understanding my message. He could not make me faithful, and did not know how to protect me from myself by saying no. He had always preferred my pleasure to his own happiness, and now, once again, his suffering would carpet the way to my delight.

Hephaestion had young Bagoas castrated, and was tender and patient with him while he healed, tolerating his insults and forgiving his attempts to murder him. One evening, when we were heading for Persepolis, he brought the youth to my tent, dressed in a eunuch's tunic.

I tore off Bagoas's clothing. Naked and backed into a corner, my captive had only his fierce emerald eyes as defense. His stare was so intense it paralyzed my desire. Instead of raping him, I held out my hand and stroked his face, which was rigid with loathing and pain. Bagoas loved me! That was why he suffered in silence. That was why he continued to appear cold and rebellious when his skin burned and moaned beneath my fingers. To prove my love for him, I put his tunic back on and sent him away.

I waited an eternity for Bagoas to come to me, and I waited another before he admitted he had desired me from our very first meeting. I did everything I could to make him a willing prisoner. He was a proud, tormented creature who showed me all the agonies of carnal passion. Bagoas was a wild bird I had forced into a gilded cage. He sang happily when he felt love, and raged for his lost manhood when hatred washed back over him. He dreamed up a thousand different ways to torture me. He told me Darius had let him mount him and had called him Little Bee. He chirped like a sparrow but refused to talk of his parents or homeland. One moment he would grovel at my feet, begging me to touch him; the next he would disappear for days on end, suffering and weeping over his infirmity. I was subjected to his mood swings and his determination to die, unable to impose my authority. His constant outbursts infuriated me, but as soon as he was away from me I missed his childlike voice, his honeyed skin, the blue shadows under his eyes, and the trace of tears on his cheeks. The Great Alexander capitulated, and Bagoas was given a place in my life: he oversaw my clothes and my meals. He was jealous of anyone close to me and complained that the Macedonians were brutal and the Greeks crude. He swept aside all rivals by intoxicating me with sensual delights of the Orient.

We headed east, then west, then north, then east again. Following the steep roads along which Darius had fled, I took cities by storm. To those that surrendered without resistance I gave their autonomy, setting up a garrison. I had scarcely arrived before I set off again, shield in hand, lance borne aloft. I no longer stopped to rest, there was not time. Towns, villages, fortresses, and fortifications reeled past, their names becoming confused. To simplify matters I called them all Alexandria. Every city that I embraced became my bride, but once married they were immediately abandoned.

The road forked in the mountains, and I always bore left. I sometimes rode for days on end, spurred on by my desire to advance ever faster. Sometimes, as I looked down on the deep valleys and torrential rivers beneath my feet, I thought of that young girl in red waiting for me at the summit of a rock. Where was she? Had I missed her by skirting round the mountain to the left? I smiled bitterly at the thought that she might be on a path I had already trodden, in a land I had already conquered.

Days of exultation alternated with times of despondency and sadness. I would shut myself away in my tent, refusing anyone entry. I wrote letter after letter to Olympias, one minute accusing her of failing to love me, the next praising her as the light of life. My mother was my only link with Macedonia, which grew a little more distant in my thoughts every day.

The road wound on through the endless snow. Only the barbarians' furs could protect us from the biting cold, and my Macedonian generals were forced to wear oriental clothes. In the evenings we lit large campfires, and the successive feast days of all the different tribes called for banquets, drinking, frenetic dancing, sacrifices, and incantations.

One morning Bessos, a Persian general, delivered Darius's body to me, an event that caused jubilation throughout the army but chilled me to the bone. A final victory without a battle is, for Alexander, a defeat. I leaned over my enemy's mutilated body, unable to accept that he was dead. Late in the night, while my soldiers slept, I came back secretly with Bagoas. Darius's former lover confirmed my doubts: this was the body of a double. Darius the coward was renouncing his throne by sending me his body: he wanted to live safely and to deprive me indefinitely of a face-to-face dual. "Dead," he hoped to pacify me with his cities and his lovers. Alive, he would remain a latent threat: he could always reappear, avenge himself, and take back what had belonged to him, what he had temporarily lost.

I pretended to fall into the trap by arranging a royal funeral for his double. I made the most of his "death" to take the pompous title of King of Asia. On the pretext that every Persian province had to submit to Alexander, I set off again along those steep roads to find the real Darius. Tracking a man who no longer existed, I ventured deeper and deeper into the shadows of the Orient.

I climbed every mountain, guided by eagles. They were not afraid of the cold or of solitude, flying high above life. Standing on those peaks, looking down at the world, I smiled to think I could die in the next battle . . . but Darius would have survived me. He would be the conqueror in a war in which he had been conquered.

. . .

BESSOS, DARIUS'S ACCOMPLICE, was flayed alive, and now no one but Bagoas knew my rival was still alive.

The world fell apart, and the world was reborn. Where there had been a narrow path, a wide road defended by garrisons appeared. In the wake of my army, inns cropped up and prospered, and caravans came and went, selling the West and buying up the East. My troops formed a thread stretching out across the land, coiling back, tumbling down hillsides and undulating

along mountain crests. Still we marched on, my legend traveling before me and most tribes choosing to surrender without
resistance. My army had grown: the soldiers from the League
of Corinth had been joined by Persian recruits and warriors offered by vassal clans. I ordered them to take local wives and sow
in their bellies the seeds of future warriors for my empire. I sent
for scholars from Greece and Babylon to accompany me in my
explorations. They were to study these hitherto unknown lands,
their fauna and their peoples, to draw them and write about
them. The blacksmiths and armorers worked nonstop. After
each battle, traders who specialized in selling weapons gathered
up enemy arsenals to supply us with the pots, fabrics, and furs
we needed. Tailors and seamstresses traveled in my footsteps to
clothe my army. Macedonian cobblers assisted by oriental slaves
supplied us with tens of thousands of pairs of sandals and shoes
whose soles wore away with the endless marching. I drew up a
contract with tomb raiders: they gave me half of their gains and
secretly sent the treasure to Ecbatana, where Parmenion managed our supplies.

Despite my glorious title of King of Asia, I slept on a carpet
on the bare earth like my soldiers, and like them I took only two
meals a day: at dawn we had bread, honey, and dried fruits; late
in the afternoon, as the sun skimmed behind the treetops, cooked
vegetables, broth, and meat. I allowed myself alcohol and copi-
ous meals only on feast days, when all those who followed me—
soldiers from every land—were invited to share in these dishes.

The fighting was so easy that the long march became wearying.
Veterans who had followed me for eight years grew homesick,
and their discontent crept up to the ranks of my generals. Not

daring to cross me publicly, they sent Hephaestion to ask me one simple question: When do we go home?

Maintaining command of such a huge army was weighing on me. Much time was lost in discussions over its administration, and the moment the fighting ceased, intrigues flourished in court once more. Having set out to conquer, I found myself a king with countless menial responsibilities, making me a slave to my own subjects. The accumulated irritations eventually drained my enthusiasm for this unprecedented spree of victories: I was filled with doubt.

When Hephaestion pressed me, I invented a justification:

"Darius is dead, but those faithful to him still resist us as if he were alive. Until I have pacified the Persian territories in their entirety, there could be revolts, towns we have already conquered could turn against us, the Achemenides nobility could betray us. We must flush out those who will not submit and exterminate every last one of them."

I could not admit to him that I missed the exultation of war, that at twenty-eight I was covered in scars and sometimes longed for rest and the sweet pleasures of family life. But a living Darius was a poison dripping stealthily into my thoughts. I could not reveal this truth to my friends, who believed I was already victorious: I am tracking a rival who confronts my strength with his cunning; he and I are competing in a trial of endurance and perseverance. Darius's flight drew me inexorably in his pursuit.

"There is no room for discussion," I told him yet again. "We must advance!"

Hephaestion withdrew sadly. He had long since stepped aside for Bagoas, who had seen him as a rival and done everything to distance him from me. The young eunuch had put on weight, like a Persian cat fattening up the moment it was well treated. Other younger and more beautiful boys had taken his place in my bedchamber. Their bodies might be slender or solid, tall or small, sometimes sculpted by exercise, their eyes might be green, brown, blue, or tawny, alive with passion or intelligence . . . they were like so many landscapes drawing me onward and appeasing me. But Bagoas was still my favorite because there was no official replacement for him in my heart. Since I had been called Alexander the Great, surrounded by courtesans, eunuchs, and guards, I had lost my appetite for love. My one constancy was Olympias, a diffuse light, an outpost that still answered my missives. I had become impatient and irascible.

Riding the umpteenth stallion called Bucephalus, I saw my abandoned past reeling out behind me. From an illegitimate girl, I had revealed myself a man. From weakness, I had acquired strength. My fear of Philip and the pain of rape had allowed me to build a life on revenge. By putting myself at the forefront of my attacks on every city, I had made myself the king of kings, leading men who were taller, more adept, and stronger than myself. I had lived intensely, wasting nothing of the lessons Aristotle taught me. I had done nothing to disappoint the gods who adopted me.

My courage was now legendary. My strength had been crowned with glory. My determination had taken me to heights forbidden to the sons of men. All these earthly rewards did nothing to gratify me. I was no longer happy.

How could I forget that Hephaestion, Bagoas, and all my friends and lovers created an invisible rampart condemning me to endless sterile solitude? How could I forget that glory was short-lived, that death might take me naked, with no crown and no lands but only regrets?

What was missing, and painfully so, was a wife who could accompany me on my journeys and through my life. What was missing was a child to whom I could pass on the ring of command. The absence of a family weakened me. The conspiracies around me multiplied, all with a view to assassinating a king with no heir.

A constant stream of young men appeared, to charm me. I saw this as an insidious maneuver intended to keep me from women. I used these boys and threw them away, convinced they had been sent to sound me out, to watch me and fill my free moments. Somewhere behind them was a man planning to take hold of my army and my empire.

I sat on my throne alone, and said nothing.

•　•　•

IT STARTED AS a slanderous rumor. Then it grew, borne on the wind, spreading through the air like pollen. People whispered that I had belittled myself by dressing as a Persian and forming an attachment for a slave like Bagoas. They said I had sunk into the arms of luxury and wasted nights on end cavorting with Darius's concubines. They said I had developed a liking for the trappings of the Great Kings and insisted my advisers and guards prostrate themselves at my feet.

Not satisfied with spreading word of my preference for men among the Macedonians, my detractors persuaded the barbarian soldiers that Alexander had contracted an evil spirit while crossing the dark, shady Drangiane region. However fiercely I punished the gossipmongers to snuff out the defamation, the rumor persisted, nesting among the soldiers wearied by endless marching but flying away as soon as it was touched. As I had no concrete proof, nothing to indicate a particular enemy hiding in the shadows, I waited patiently.

Eventually the huge conspiracy fell apart, quite by chance. An officer called Dymnus became infatuated with a prostitute known as Nicomachus. He confided in him his plan to assassinate me and invited the boy to join him and the other conspirators. Nicomachus was quick to denounce him to his brother Cebalinus, who in turn spoke to Philotas, who had access to my private tent. Philotas was the son of Parmenion, a general to whom I had entrusted the command of Media and the management of our supplies, but he was careful not to warn me of the danger.

Cebalinus eventually reached me himself and gave me the names of the parricidal plotters. But Philotas's silence struck me as more dangerous than a few little foot soldiers dreaming of killing their king. It proved that he wished me dead.

Everything became clear to me then: Parmenion, Philotas's father, was the man hiding in the shadows and slowly turning the army against me! I made Crateros responsible for subjecting Philotas to torture. His cries rang out, filling me with self-loathing. I could picture him in one of his languid poses and could not bear the thought that he only loved me the better to betray me.

His father Parmenion, now seventy years old, had once enjoyed Philip's respect and Olympias's friendship. He had come over to my camp after Philip's death by executing my rival Attalus. He had used his skills as an orator to rally the Greeks, and his strategies had seen me win many battles. Two of his sons had died in combat, and he had offered me the vigorous young flesh of his last son. Blinded by this evidence of his support, I had interpreted his ambiguity as flexibility, his eloquence as sincerity, and his opportunism as loyalty.

The old man was a monster; why had it taken me so long to see?

He went to every banquet and invited himself into all the taverns, befriending the Persian nobility to build up his network. He waited until I reached the remotest regions of Persia to launch rumors that disrupted my soldiers. He arranged for supplies of food to arrive late or be lost along the way. Hunger and cold angered my commanders, and they too started criticizing me and plotting against me. Parmenion was a fine strategist; he could have eliminated me without touching a weapon. As governor of Media he could have taken over my empire without taking part in any conspiracy.

This ploy would have been the perfect crime, but the gods decided otherwise. The moment Philotas's confession was ripped from him, I sent a well-chosen man to take a letter to Parmenion announcing a promotion. The general who dreamed of becoming King of Asia greeted my message with delight. He was stabbed on the spot; the strategist had lost thanks to his own strategies.

.   .   .

THE STEEP MOUNTAINS softened and curved; the hills turned to plains covered in meadowland. Despite warnings from my Persian generals, who still remembered defeats inflicted by the nomads, despite complaints from the Macedonians, who wanted to go home, I unleashed an arrow toward the sun and my army advanced into the kingdom of the Scythians.

Every country has its own ocean. The steppes were the Mediterranean of the northern peoples. The whispering of leaves replaced the murmur of waves. As seagulls cluster around ships, so here blackbirds flew up into the sky singing of heroes who died for glory and for love. The Scythian tribes, renowned for their savagery and insolence, appeared and vanished around us. Their mounted warriors and skilled archers attacked us and then withdrew. They loomed on the horizon like a pack of starving wolves, stole food, took women and children, then—like thunderclouds fleeing to reveal blue skies—dispersed.

"The steppes are haunted, and these tribes have powerful sorcerers," the Persians muttered, trying to discourage me. "During their ceremonies, these men dress in lion skins and adorn themselves with feathers, animal teeth, and mirrors. They beat drums and sing and dance until they collapse, foaming at the mouth and rolling their eyes. Then the earth ripples and opens up to swallow foreign troops while the spirits of dead soldiers come down from the sky."

I learned that Darius had been here before me. Nothing could stop me in my headlong pursuit of him. If the enemy fled across the steppe, then why should I, Alexander, not face its shifting vastness and elusive horsemen in my turn?

The wind whispered, the wind howled. Unhindered, the sky spilled over the four horizons. Some soldiers, oppressed by the vastness, went mad. They threw off their clothes and ran screaming from the encampment. The Persians explained that, unable to find houses to live in, the spirits wandered day and night over these lands, without rest. When they met foreigners not protected by magic formulae, they took possession of their souls. I thought nothing of their superstitions but doubled the number of guards watching over our camps because I knew that at night the nomads could disguise themselves as spirits to sow terror in my army.

I heard tell that on the banks of the Iaxarte there was an annual market that drew all the tribes together, and that the previous year, Darius had been seen there. He had become a flamethrower, and the crowd applauding him had no idea he had once been king of kings.

Before I arrived, the nomads had taken down their tents and disappeared. All that was left on the ground were the holes where they had planted their stakes, and chariot tracks almost washed away by the rain. The river reflected the blue sky. I was accustomed to conquering cities and attacking fortresses on steep rocks, and for the first time I was overcome by how strange life was on the steppe. I had not come through a single town or met a single inhabitant. I could see no villages or roads on my map. Wherever I went, the horizons were empty and the inhabitants vanished. Only the grasses with their constant whispering seemed to want to communicate to me the cries of joy and animated conversations of those people. But where are the tribes? Where are my enemies? Where are the people I should subjugate and who should proclaim me as their king? Who are these people that they are indifferent to Alexander and don't come to meet him in war?

Has Darius learned to be invisible? Has he come to the steppes in search of the magic that allowed men to melt into the wind?

I could no longer bear the weight of my army on my shoulders or the slow pace of our progress: I silenced their displeasure and their nostalgia by ordering them to set up camp and rest. I myself took a detachment and headed north.

I abandoned my demoralized troops with a sense of relief, galloping toward the skies like a bird escaping a trap.

. . .

THE HORIZON DREW closer. The vast swell of grasses threw itself in the air and closed in again. With every wave conquered, another impetuous wave rose up. I slid deeper into their dark ocean, forgetting sunlight, thirst, and hunger. What I truly forgot were the traitors and the complainers, their constant appetite for booty and their intriguing for glory. I called to Hephaestion to advance even faster. With speed I would conquer this vastness. With strength I would subjugate the infinite and transform it into the finite.

The sun set and the moon rose. The stars revolved and dawn came back again. Under the reddening sky, the darkness was an army beating the retreat. As I galloped onward I heard laughter and murmuring. The spirits were close by me now, mocking my progress. Their singing! The incantations of those invisible peoples trying to slow my pace, to frighten Bucephalus. Be gone, evil spirits!

Hephaestion was exhausted. He fell ill, and I had to stop. He ranted for a whole night: like a woman determined to take her warrior home, he was trying desperately to drag me back the way we had come.

"Alexander who has triumphed over every mountain peak shall not be defeated by the steppe," I explained.

The next morning I did not wake him but left him with half my soldiers while I carried on northward.

One day at dawn some impoverished nomads driving a flock of sheep appeared. They greeted me in their language, welcomed me into their tent, invited me to eat and drink and offered their wives and daughters for my bed. They did not know who I was. They were not troubled by the absence of dialogue, and I managed to speak in gestures. I asked many of them the same question: Where are the outer limits of the steppes? and they all replied: In the stars.

We rode on together. I met other tribes, some made up of only ten people. They lived in poor, flimsy tents and vanished without warning, leaving us adrift on the green waves. Their sorcerers dressed in robes of leather and lion skin, they danced and sang and raved until they looked liked wolves, bears, or eagles and delivered their oracles. They could not write, and they healed the sick using magic potions and formulae. They smiled a great deal and took us for a warrior tribe.

I forgot Pella and Olympias and her marble palace. I forgot Athens and its ruined temples. I forgot Babylon, its scarlet walls, its tall chambers filled with incense. I forgot the burned citadels, the conquered towns, my argument with Cleitos and his body pierced by my lance. I had left them all to be with the wind, the spirits, and the green waves.

I navigated ever northward. I was no longer Alexander but the chief of a small nomadic tribe. The moon had a different luminosity, watching me and smiling. That evening it spoke:

"Alexander, prepare yourself! The volcano is about to spew out a storm of stars, the sun will come to meet the moon! Pack away your tent, pack your trunks. She is coming, she will capture you. She will take you away!"

The following morning an army appeared on the horizon.

. . .

AT FIRST IT was a line of black, then short silhouettes on broad sturdy horses. They became minute warriors wearing painted armor and helmets adorned with feathers. Their arrows rained down on us; one burrowed into my shoulder, another into my horse's neck. It was a very long time since I had been in battle. The pain awakened Alexander as he slept. My own body unfurled, and Bucephalus, spurred on by his blood, reared and whinnied. Dashing aside arrows with my shield, I sped toward the enemy with a roar.

One of their number launched himself at me. He held off my lance with a long-handled bludgeon covered in spines, while with the sickle in his left hand he cleaved into the bronze plate and seven layers of leather on my shield. I pushed it at him, and he flung it in the air with a swipe of his bludgeon. My left hand found my sword in its sheath; I threw myself forward, aiming for his head. My lance crossed his bludgeon. My bronze sword, inherited from Philip and blessed by Vulcan, clashed with his sickle. A deafening sound. Sparks. The sickle had just chipped Alexander's invincible two-edged sword!

On his chest, over his darned red tunic, this barbarian warrior wore a strange glinting black panel. There was a furious face painted on it, and as he moved, it became a bird with pointed teeth and golden talons at the ends of its wings. He wore a helmet topped with an eagle's head and adorned with long white feathers.

He was riding bareback on a chestnut mare much smaller than Bucephalus but so nimble-footed she hovered round my stallion like a bee, avoiding his charges then coming back to brush past him, biting him, then fleeing.

The warrior's sharp weapons flew and flashed around me. When they struck my sword, their sharp cries rang out like the anguished wails of a starving beast. The face painted on the black panel laughed derisively, trying to frighten me. The eagle-headed helmet hid his forehead and eyes, which appeared as two black flames dancing languidly and apparently talking to me of love.

In previous combat, when I looked my enemy in the eye I read death, not love. Was this stranger trying to bewitch me? His bludgeon suddenly broke my lance, and my rage exploded: I threw off the combination of sentimentality, pity, and admiration I had felt for the hardened and audacious young barbarian. My sword whistled through the air, and, unable to withstand my powerful blows, he retreated. As Bucephalus charged on the mare, my weapon touched the panel covering the warrior's breast. Sparks flew. A furious noise like the roar of a wounded tiger almost deafened me and stunned the barbarian. When he recovered his composure, he turned his horse and fled.

I understood from what he was wearing and from the standing of his weapons that he was chief of this warrior tribe. All those who gave offense to Alexander had to choose between capitulation and death. I set off in pursuit of him.

Even though she was small, the chestnut mare sped across the steppe like a star. Aroused by the long mane that she shook vigorously, Bucephalus galloped behind. At first, arrows continued to whistle past: my soldiers and the barbarian warriors were still fighting as they tried to follow us. Then, silence. Then, the trembling speed. Then I was carried on the wind. I could hear nothing but its wailing.

. . .

THE SUN SET. A truce.

The warrior had set up camp a hundred paces or so away. He built a fire and ate. I nibbled on some dried bread from my pouch and lay down on the grass with my sword in my hand. I closed my eyes, but my ears remained open, alert to my rival's movements.

Before dawn he set off again at a gallop. I whistled to Bucephalus, who launched into his frenetic pursuit once more. The sun rose and poured its orange light over the steppe, making millions of dewdrops roll and glisten on the grass. Birds frightened by the horses flew off in a beating of wings, leaving their calling, cooing, and trilling behind.

On the third day the warrior stopped fleeing, and we fought from morning till night. I did not know where he found his inexhaustible strength, but his attacks were not so aggressive. I returned this mark of courtesy, careful not to injure him. Night fell, and the crescent moon rose. I lay watching the stars with my hands behind my head. The last time I had looked closely at them had been fifteen years ago, when I was still a boy full of dreams who knew nothing of the hard combat and noisy conquests inscribed in my destiny. I had still been rich with my own loneliness, unfamiliar with the plots of generals, the banter of eunuchs, or the luxurious laughter of courtesans. My eyes had not been invaded by towns, roads, corpses, and lovers' naked bodies; nor my ears sullied by rumors, accusations, arguments, and the clamor of war. That is why I could see the stars and understand their language. I had lost touch with the sky to delve into the world of men. Now, with the challenge laid down by this unknown warrior, I had left behind my soldiers, the last men who tied me to the tumultuous life of a king.

In the sky, dark eyes sparkled among the stars, talking of love, not death.

On the fourth day a group of nomadic horsemen appeared, like monsters uprooted from the depths of the ocean. They glided closer on the crests of those green waves. Without explanation, they plied toward us, screaming, weapons raised. The unknown warrior rode straight at these men, though they were much taller than him, like an intrepid young wolf throwing itself on a horde of starving hyenas. I fell in step with him, and together we forged a path for ourselves.

The screams of those once fierce horsemen faded and disappeared.

Ahead of me, the warrior continued to gallop. I no longer had any reason to want his death or his submission. I was following him for the competition, curious to see which of us was the stronger, had the better endurance.

On the fifth night there was no moon and the wind stirred. I woke with a start: a pair of eyes shone in the darkness in front of me. The young man was standing in the tall grass, and we fought on foot. During this struggle I managed to hoist off his helmet, and my hand grasped his thick hair. I pulled with all my strength; the savage leapt at me and bit me ferociously on the neck. At dawn the next day he mounted his mare and set off again at a gallop. I chased after him without even wondering why. Our horses sped across the steppes, accompanied by flocks of birds fluttering out of the bushes.

I held in my hand a long hank of smooth black hair, floating on the wind. I would go to the very edge of this terrestrial world, I would go where this young barbarian could no longer flee. He would let me disarm him, I, Alexander, who wished only love for him, not hatred.

But love weakened me, and during the course of the day I was overwhelmed by sadness. Philip loomed in my thoughts, Philip in flesh and blood, holding me in his arms, against his phallus. Olympias stood on the edge of her terrace where the orange trees blossomed and gazed at the horizon over which I had left her forever. I saw Hephaestion as a youth, wanting to leave Macedonia with a medicine man to forget my disloyal heart. I had kept him there with my tears, abusing his gentleness but never promising him anything. Other boys came to mind, furtive loves met in taverns or loved for one night after the glories of battle. They were followed by Persian slaves who had offered me their bodies, and Bagoas, whose love for life I had castrated. I had conquered and raped everything. I had submitted men and women to the strength of my lance. Every city that bore my name and every soldier dead in my name had further fanned the flames of fury in me. Alexander, king of Asia, had driven out the other Alexander, the reader of stars who had loved a philosopher, his flaccid body, his considered words, his calm mind, and his world without wars.

That night as I gazed at the stars I started singing a Macedonian washerwoman tune that I had not thought of once through all the years of campaigning. My voice floated on the silence, burrowed through the rustling grasses, and reemerged, accompanied by a higher voice. In the distance the barbarian was singing a sad melody in his own language. Our two voices followed and outran each other, mingling together and rising toward the stars.

When I opened my eyes again, it was morning. I saw the face of a young boy, huge as he leaned right over me. He had two long black braids and the high cheekbones of the people of the steppes; the slanting line of his eyes reached his temples, and there was a scar on his chin.

I gave an involuntary cry:

"You're a spirit!"

His eyes seemed to question the meaning of my words. I tried to use a word I had learned from the nomads:

"You're a *cheugoul*!"

He smiled. He nicked the top of my chest with the tip of his sickle. I shuddered. This was not a dream! I recognized his scarlet tunic, his black eyes, and his mare grazing close by with Bucephalus. I slid my hand discreetly toward my sword but touched the sharpened spines of his bludgeon.

"What's your name?" I asked in a friendly voice.

He did not seem to understand my accent, learned from a different tribe to his. He raised his weapon again and laid it over my throat. I was not afraid of death. I was used to the cold surface of a blade. I stared right into my tormentor's eyes, challenging him. He moved closer to me abruptly and put his lips to mine. The instincts of a man accustomed to combat tensed my every muscle; I struggled and pushed him away. He stood back up and put two fingers into his mouth to whistle for his mare; she came over, followed by Bucephalus. He mounted his horse; I got on my stallion. He threw himself into the limitless steppes; I galloped by his side toward the sky.

• • •

CLOUDS SCUDDED BY, gradually tinged with yellow, blue, pink, and orange, then brilliant red. Birds as swift as arrows sped noisily toward the sun, which had just dropped to the horizon. We galloped behind them, heading right into the sun blazing with flames and aglow with light. The vermilion hills wavered and turned to rivers, mountains, giant trees reaching their branches up to the burning red sky. The sun's heart was a lake of boiling crimson lava. White creatures appeared and ripped away my past like a tattered old robe, then vanished in the incandescent waters.

Night fell, and we lit a fire. The boy eyed me through the flames.

"What's your name?" I asked again.

"I am Alestria," he told me, "and you?"

I hesitated.

"Are you a man or a woman?" he asked me.

His question amused me.

"I'm a man, and you?"

"You, a man? I don't believe you."

Amazed by his reply, I repeated myself to remove any possibility of misunderstanding:

"I am a man, a man!"

He leaped up and jumped over the fire, pushing me to the ground and putting his hand between my legs.

"*Zougoul!*" he cried in horror and fled toward his horse.

I was astonished, watching him leave in the darkness but unable to react. It was a dark night, and the grasshoppers wept softly. Shadows had engulfed the steppes, for the young warrior had disappeared and taken all my joy with him. I vaulted onto Bucephalus and set off to find him.

I drifted across the steppe, calling Alestria. Wolves answered my calls, and their solitary howls pierced right through my heart. Why did you run from me, Alestria? Were you deceived by my curly hair, my fine features that have lent their beauty to sculptors in every country? Are you looking for a wife, Alestria? I would be as gentle as a girl, I, Alexander, who was Olympias's daughter and Philip's wife!

Come back, Alestria!

. . .

A BLACK SILHOUETTE outlined against a wide ribbon of silver. Alestria had stopped before a river: it blocked his way so he could not escape me. Such was the will of the gods and the *cheugouls*. I went over to him and took him in my arms. We threw down our weapons and fell to the ground, rolling in the grass, lips against lips, breast against breast, our legs intertwined . . . but Alestria was a woman!

A woman who knew how to fight!

A woman who had taken Alexander from his men!

A woman who had fled me but been returned to me by the will of the gods!

Tears spilled from my eyes, though I could not have said why. Soon my own body gave me the explanation: it had found the other half lost when it fell from the skies. My hands, arms, hips, stomach, the backs of my knees, the tips of my toes . . . all slotted into the contours that had been waiting to make a whole with them. They embraced and knotted together, becoming a tree with roots spreading over the steppe, plunging into rivers, and climbing up to the sky.

. . .

I WAS WOKEN the following morning by birdsong, and found myself lying naked surrounded by hundreds of wildflowers. The sun was peeping over the horizon, pouring a layer of red light over the steppes. My eyes searched for Alestria: she had gone again! My head swam, and I leaped to my feet. Standing beside the river, I could make out a dark shape in the water. I called to her. She turned and waved to me from a distance, then vanished among the blinding sparkles and reappeared below me, shaking her head and sending out a shower of droplets.

"*Talas!*" she cried.

I knew neither how to swim nor how to tell her I could not.

"*Talas*, come!"

She climbed out of the water and came over to me. Her body was that of a warrior: her breasts, hips, and thighs gleamed and were marked with long scars and deep wounds like trophies. Her black braids shone in the sunlight and hung down to her navel. Her wet face was like a child's, with full lips and cheeks tanned by the sun. She threw her arms around me and held me to her till I shivered at the touch of her icy skin.

"*Talas!*" she cried, running toward the river.

I did not know how to swim. But I had no choice but to

follow her. I ran into the water and sank like a stone. The waves surrounded me. The river was a bed of flowers: magnolias, dahlias, carnations, roses, and violets bloomed around me. I moved forward and reached out to pick them. My body felt light and rose up from the riverbed, flying toward the sky: yes, I was flying, beating my hands, which had turned into wings. I slid among silvery fish and avenues of undulating weeds. At the far end of the path the sun was no longer an incandescent ball of fire but a face floating over a vault of shadows and reflections. All of a sudden it became wrinkled, and its expression changed. I saw Alestria moving back and forth: she was looking for me! I wanted to swim toward her, but the current stopped me reaching her, and I was carried farther away. I wanted to call her name, but water poured into my mouth. I lost sight of her silhouette, and the sun disappeared. My eyes were filled with beams of yellow, orange, pink, purple, and crimson, which turned into a rainbow.

· · ·

I OPENED MY eyes and saw Alestria's chin and chest. My head was resting in her hands on her lap. Her melancholic gaze fixed the horizon. Although she was naked, she seemed to be wrapped in a magnificent veil made neither of fabric nor fur but of a corner of sky pierced with flashes of lightning. She looked down and stared into my eyes. Her dark eyes seemed to be questioning me: "Will you dare to lay down your weapons and love a little savage? Will you dare take a vagabond with you on your noble Bucephalus? You, Alexander, son of Philip, king of kings, conqueror of the

Greeks, and of Olympias, daughter of Achilles and Zeus, will you dare to make this child your queen, this child abandoned by men and by the gods?"

I said nothing, but met her gaze.

No, I would not hesitate.

The king of conquerors was not afraid of a warrior woman. He recognized in her someone who had been banished from those kingdoms with ten thousand palaces and one hundred thousand downy cushions; she was a brother living in a stranger's body, a spiritual sister carved from the same block of diamond.

No, I would not hesitate. My pride would be disarmed, the invincible warrior would be vanquished. Wait a little longer! Let me gather my strength in silence and prepare to welcome in the love about to strike my life like a thunderbolt.

She was my queen! Without any doubt. Her melancholy calm, her spontaneous joy, and her black eyes reflecting all the mysteries of Asia displayed more majesty than those capricious princesses who were never exposed to the sun. My eye slid down her neck to her naked breasts, and on the inside of her left breast, I discovered a large scar, a terrifying emblem. I could not tell whether her flesh had been deeply scored by a dagger or marked by a white-hot iron. The crimson skin that had grown over the wound was marked with lines and calluses, and I imagined that she positioned the bound rope of her bow there.

I laid my hand on the scar. She sat up with a start and wanted to flee, but I rolled on top of her and pinned her down with the weight of my body. I rested my face on her injured breast and heard her heart beating.

Alestria, your origins do not matter: whether you are a free warrior or a fighting slave, I shall take you from your tribe and free you from servitude.

Alestria, child of the steppes, you have conquered the invincible Alexander! For you he will stop scouring conquered lands in search of a noblewoman worthy of being his queen.

Alestria, you who do not know my name, I who do not know your parents' names, we shall found our own dynasty. Alexander and Alestria: from our two names combined a river will spring up and flow to the very ends of humanity.

What does it matter that you have neither clothes nor jewels nor a kingdom? All that is Alexander's is yours: he offers you his army, his cities, his empire! You will lay down your arms, he will wage wars for you.

You will be my companion in my travels and in my life. Together we shall ride to the ends of the earth. All my suffering will be relegated to the past. All your suffering will be erased.

Alestria, I love you! I offer you Alexander, whose beauty is nothing compared to his ability to love. I offer you diamonds, sapphires, rubies, and the most luxurious fabrics to make you the youngest, most beautiful, and most glorious queen on earth.

You were destined for me, Alestria! It is I, the most powerful of men, whom the gods have chosen for you to tear you from the shadows and make you shine in the zenith!

Oh, Alestria, give me your wounds and your weapons. All those who have possessed you and all those you have loved shall be exiled! I have come to take you, to take you away!

Come, Alestria, my love! I came onto this earth for you. Together we shall ride to the firmament. Do not refuse me!

A thousand years, ten thousand years, from now the birds

on the steppe will still sing of our meeting: on a moonless night two stars collide, the sky burns and spews out a tempest of flames and lightning. Every legend already written shall be burned, and a new era shall rise up from their ashes!

CHAPTER 6

My name is not Alestria, it is Talestria: the T represents the tribe of Amazons, the women who love horses.

I do not know when I was born.

I like red, the color of leaves burned by the sun, the color of blood.

I do not know who my parents were.

On the steppe countless men and women love each other for one night and then part without the promise of meeting again in another life.

On the steppe, every encounter has the intensity of a fleeting moment, for it is as easy to be born as it is to die. Life is as brief as one passing season, spanning one torrential rainstorm, the tiny moment it takes a bird to reach the clouds.

One beauty erases another; they are all ephemeral.

Talestria is queen of the Amazons. I knew that this name, like all other names I had been given, would be short-lived. I wore it like a piece of armor to go into war. One day I would leave it just as I came to it, anonymous and without weapons.

Our tribe was made up of girls without a past, all of them abandoned orphans. Each taken in by the warrior tribe, we in turn became women who feared nothing: cold, war, and famine were the three eagles sent to us by the God of Ice to guide us to the summit of Siberia.

"The greatest good comes through the greatest evil," my aunt used to say.

That is why my life started so badly: a little girl with no name who slipped into every name she was attributed. Her face was dirty, her features hard, her lips wizened with cold and thirst. Her hair, which was never cut, looked like a swallow's nest with locks trailing over her face, hiding her fierce expression. She strayed through the marketplace, her cracked, bleeding hands stealing the occasional piece of fruit or biscuit, or squeezing a goat's udder for a mouthful of milk. She threw stones at children who laughed at her, and hid under carts when dogs chased her, lying in manure and beating their snapping jaws back with a stick. But adults were more dangerous and cruel than dogs, dragging her through the dusty alleyways and whipping her. She suffered their blows without a sob, sometimes even laughing to please them. She wanted to live and to avenge herself; that is why she disguised her rage and chose to appear docile.

She wandered around the marketplace, not knowing where she came from or who her parents were. She let families adopt her, and for a couple of seasons she played the role of a good-natured, servile slave. They would give her a name, a plate, and a blanket that she shared with sheep, calves, and fleas. Then she would run away and escape to the steppes, running through the grass that was taller than she was, diving into rivers and letting the currents carry her off, floating on her back watching clouds and birds go by. At night she shivered, hungry and exhausted, with only the howling of wolves as comfort; she knew how to call to them to warm her and lick her wounds.

A new family came on horseback and took her. One evening, beside the fire, she heard the legend of the Amazons. The following morning at dawn she stole some food and slipped out of the tent. She crossed the steppe on foot, walking into the wind and the snow, following the stars, which sang to her:

Night is the light of day
Night is the light of the earth
Night is the key to treasure
You must come through the night to reach the day
You must follow the stars to reach the sun
Every footstep takes you toward the white cranes with crimson
  heads
Every night of walking brings you closer to the warrior woman
  brandishing two weapons
Every day counts
Days are counted
You have to want
Walk and you will see
Count the days to give yourself strength
Count the days when you weep

When you are happy forget about time
When you suffer count the days

Bird of the glacier, fly toward the light!
Bird of the Glacier, fly toward the sun!
Fly toward your god!

My name is Talestria. Talestria, meaning "the joys of combat."

My mother's name was Talaxia, "scarlet feather."

I am queen of the girls of Siberia, who thirst for happiness: laughing makes us forget death.

I know nothing of tiredness.

I would not weep if my beloved sisters died tomorrow.

Suffering has carved a deep pit in my heart for life to pour its loveliness into.

War is an evil; happiness is my combat.

The girls of Siberia love war; they also love to enjoy themselves and laugh.

Sadness would wash over us after nightfall when, in the middle of a rowdy feast, the girls started to sing. Our god was music; he had engendered words, words had engendered thought, and thought had set women free. Our songs were earthly melodies that had to reach for the skies like birds. I would weep; all the girls would: music reopened our wounds and resuscitated our dead.

War purified us; our enemies' blood wiped from our breasts the memories of little girls crying in despair.

Why was I chosen by the warrior women? Why was I their queen? Why, when my mother took me in, did she appoint me as her heir? Everyone here believed it was my destiny. Everyone except for me.

I bore a scar on my left breast. All Amazons bear a deep welt on one of their breasts to position the leather strap of their bows. Mine was a wound, but I no longer remember how it happened.

I wanted to remember only happy moments from my previous life: running through the market holding steaming hot bread in my hand; jumping up to catch a dragonfly; dancing round a fire while in the shadows eyes watched me and hands clapped out the rhythm as I spread my arms and twirled, flew, reached the very stars.

I, Talestria, was born and became queen the day my mother Talaxia's body was brought back to the camp. In her left breast was an arrow topped with blue and green feathers.

I was brought up by my mother's servant, whom I called my aunt. Her name was Tankiasis, "the fragrance of white chrysanthemum." She was strict and gentle, recounting old legends to me while she rocked me in her arms. The first time I rode a full-sized horse, she made me gallop for days on end. On my first birthday, a year after my mother had died, she gave me more weapons honed for the survival of our tribe: the language of birds, the writing in the stars, the magic of numbers, the gift of healing.

She had a little girl with white skin and golden hair. My mother, queen Talaxia, had told me:

"Tania is your sister; she will be your servant when you are queen. You will make war, and Tania will watch over the flocks. She will raise your child and will be your regent if you die in combat. She will raise a servant for the new queen and will disappear when the two little girls have become women."

Tania was silent and shy, calm but always worrying. She would back away and scream if a frog leaped up, a bird flew off, a snake spat, or a caterpillar was simply too brightly colored. She was haunted by a nightmare and she wore its terror like a tattoo: she saw herself sleeping in a bed, surrounded by soft cushions and glittering cloth, and a white breast came toward her to give her milk. When she tried to look up at the face of the woman nursing her, men loomed into view, slicing sabers through the air. Their bellowing was like the roar of thunder. One of them tore her from the breast and threw her from the window.

As Tankiasis had for Queen Talaxia, Tania and I constituted day and night. Where I was courageous, she was fearful; where I was impulsive, she was cautious; where I advanced, she retreated. In areas where I felt weak, she found her strength. Every queen of Siberia has a servant, a sister, to complement her wisdom and perfect her virtue.

For a queen must never make a mistake.

She is the survival of the tribe of warrior women.

．　．　．

IN THE TERRESTRIAL world, war is an evil. But evil applied to evil forges good.

One night I was woken by muffled screams. The pine trees outside were in flames, and sheep ran hectically past my tent, bleating in fear. Some of my sisters beat drums to warn of the men's attack, while Tankiasis was already launching herself at the warriors with a weapon in each hand. One after another the girls threw themselves into the flames. I would have liked to follow them, but Tania had been given orders to take me to a shelter dug into the ground, and all through the night we listened to the clash of weapons and whinnying horses.

Tankiasis woke us at dawn, covered in blood, wild-eyed, and stinking of warfare.

She took us by the hand and led us to the battlefield, where bushes were still burning and the ground was strewn with bodies. She ordered us to kill any man still alive.

I found a young warrior still breathing; his clothes were lacerated, and his right shoulder was completely missing. He was slumped against his panting horse, gazing at the sky as if it were the most beautiful view. When he saw me coming over, he smiled at me; he had the darkest eyes and a face as pale as a lily. He was so ravishing, with his curly hair and the blood emptying peacefully from his body! I put one knee to the ground and drew my dagger. He stared at me intently, his eyes caressing my face and carving into my heart.

In a flash I sliced his throat: his body twitched, his lips quivered. Little flames flickered and then expired in his horrified eyes. Where was he from? What was his name? What was his horse called? How often had he ridden out across the steppes?

Death is not beautiful, but there is beauty when the warrior spirit leaves a body.

I had killed my first man. I had become a woman. I too was ready to die in battle.

Men, we called them *zougouls*! I was obsessed with them!

As I walked along the banks of the Iaxarte, close to my mother and holding hands with Tankiasis, I no longer thought of men simply as adults who beat children. Now that I was an Amazon, I had learned to see them as haughty and cunning horsemen.

"When you grow up," Talaxia told me, "you will be stronger than these men."

"Males have no udder to feed their young," Tankiasis added. "They have no bellies to bear young. That is why they constantly chase females to make them bear their progeny."

"Yes," said Talaxia. "They're like walking cuckoos, laying their eggs in other birds' nests."

"Except ours!" Tankiasis laughed. "The girls of Siberia drink magic infusions. They don't lay eggs, they fly away."

Many men approached my mother, and when she spoke to them they were the ones who lowered their eyes in submission. When they fought with her naked, she was the one who forced them to the ground and mounted them.

The wind blew through the doorway, and the moonlight drifted in and out. I was fascinated by men's muscles and swore mine would be like theirs when I grew up. Talaxia was not afraid of a man taller than her; she seized him bodily, handled him roughly, turned him round. With her long hair swinging in the silvery moonbeams, a distant smile playing on her lips and her eyes pinned to the top of the glacier, my mother made the man howl, begging her to love him again.

He had stopped shouting and lay snoring. My mother called me and put my hand on his sex. It was cold and damp, disgusting.

"Our sex is in our heads," my mother told me. "No one can steal it, no one can take it away!"

My head still reeling with the feel of that man's genitals, I wandered among the market stalls with Tania. Boys dressed in blue and saffron cloth, their heads wrapped in turbans, winked and threw flowers at us. The boldest stopped us and tried to talk to us. Tania panicked and dragged me away, not wanting them to touch me, afraid they might bewitch me. She was happier watching monkeys dancing with snakes, but I broke away from her and slipped into the crowd. She ran after me, calling to me as I weaved along alleyways between bustling customers, and hid among hanging carpets and bolts of cloth. Tania was stubborn as a mule and would not give up.

Tania was afraid of men. I simply did not like them.

. . .

I WAS GROWING, and my breasts filling out. I used my bow a hundred times a day to dig a deep furrow in the wound on my left breast, and the tough scar tissue forming over it meant I could carry ever heavier bows. I chose bigger and bigger horses, compensating for my small stature with the size of my horse and perfecting my own strengths with my own sacred weapons.

Every queen of Siberia, when she reaches maturity, must travel to the land of the volcano, where she is given a gift of black blades forged by our cousins, the whale hunters. Accompanied by my faithful Tania, I covered a huge distance to reach the forest and then the ocean. I was greeted by the Great Mother of the tribe, who had a beard and many tattoos. There was a special ceremony during which she sang, surrounded by dancing women, and called on the spirits, which had indicated their desire to be incarnated in my weapons. Three seasons later, a sun-shaped bludgeon and a moon-shaped sickle were forged and beaten out on the foothills of the volcano. Two warrior souls came down to breathe life into them: the female soul wedded the solar bludgeon, the male soul the lunar sickle. During my time on the shores of that freezing ocean, the sun darkened in the very middle of the day, devoured by the moon.

"A great queen has come to earth," concluded the Great Mother, studying me closely. "The moon has outstripped the sun: a queen shall conquer a king."

I was not that queen. I would like to have told her that, but I held my tongue. I was not a queen, I was a bird of the steppes.

"The king and queen will come to the land of the volcano," she said, gazing at the glaciers that were now black shadows.

After my return we were attacked by a nomadic tribe. I gave my first orders, and my aunts and sisters followed my commands. Our attackers were ferocious men and more numerous than us, but they fell into my strategic trap. Once they were divided, we struck them down one after the other with our swift blades.

The Amazons decapitated their slain enemies and slung their heads over their horses' rumps as trophies. Some reduced them to the size of an apple and attached them to their headdresses. Others dried out the head, liver, and testicles, ground them to a powder, and used it to make an infusion that gave them strength and courage. They spoke magic incantations and buried the heart, thereby appeasing the suffering of those souls constrained to leave the valiant bodies of an indomitable tribe.

I had no adornment. The only head I would have liked to hang on a length of woven cord between my breasts was that of my first warrior. I carried the memory of him in my heart—he was my invisible jewel.

There were frequent wars on the steppe: nomadic tribes quarreled, were reconciled, stole from each other, and were allied by marriages. One tribe might be exterminated and wiped from the face of the earth; others might appear on the horizon screaming their war cries, having sprung up apparently from nowhere. There was once a tribe in which the men painted themselves blue, but we no longer saw them at the market. Then there were men with red tattoos who brought a new language, but they in turn disappeared. There had been a tribe of bird tamers and a clan of snake charmers. There was a tribe that venerated stones, and another that venerated their mothers.

On the steppes the grasses grow and dry out; men and women are born and die like the grasshoppers; the earth is inseminated by the rain and hatches new lives; war can destroy just as readily as the earth brings forth.

The tribe of girls who love horses had survived the erosion of time; it had survived massacres, the cold, and the wind. It was condemned to perish like the mountain that collapses beneath the eternal snows.

The Amazons fought for death.

Death is the black light of the life.

I wanted the golden light of the sun.

I carried in my heart the immortality of all things loved.

. . .

WHEN I WAS fourteen, I was smitten by a girl I caught sight of at the market. She had a white veil and sparkling black eyes; I could imagine her raspberry mouth, and teeth as hard as little seashells. She was surrounded by serving women, tending to her like the chick of a white bird with a red head.

From the first moment I saw her, I could not bear to be away from her. Despite Tania's supplications, I followed her for days on end, and Tania returned to the camp, exhausted. I carried on hovering around the girl until she eventually spoke to me: when she realized that I loved her, she arranged to meet me in a luxurious inn. I sold my mare to pay for that night.

Salimba undressed before I even touched her, and she threw her curvaceous body and full breasts into my arms. I loved her again and again. Between our couplings she told me she was betrothed to an ugly, cruel, and aging tribal chief, a man who already had ten wives; she would be his eleventh. She said she was unhappy, that her father also had ten wives, and that she was the tenth wife's daughter. She said that she foresaw terrible suffering, that the ten wives would speak ill of her and mistreat her, that she might just earn the tribe's respect if she bore a son, and that her daughters would be sold to men as she and her mother had been.

Salimba wept, suffocated by her fate. And so I spoke to her of white cranes with crimson heads and of our wars against men. I invited her to have a child with me and to become my wife. She stopped weeping, listening attentively with her head resting on the wound on my breast.

"I would have liked to marry you, Talestria," she said after a long silence. "But I am not an Amazon. My belly is flaccid, my legs soft, my arms have no strength, I can barely even lift a pail of water. I know neither how to cook nor to hunt nor to live without perfumed milk, nor to sleep without a thick mattress woven with ewe's wool. Forget Salimba, she is a weakling. Hold me in your arms. Love me once more, one last time!"

When dawn broke, my beloved was dressed and I helped her straighten her veil. I watched her leave along the damp alleyways of a deserted marketplace. I never saw Salimba again. The following year I heard that she had had a sumptuous wedding and was expecting a child. The year after that I was told that she had borne a daughter, and that she was with child again. The next year her name was no longer spoken; she was dead.

We frequently came across corpses on the steppes. They might be our sisters or our enemies, and any one of them could have been Salimba. I addressed to each of them a prayer to appease their soul, wishing them a happy incarnation in lives to come.

"Tankiasis," I said, "we cannot form an attachment with a man and give him a child, but why can we not wed a woman and conceive with her? Two women together make girl children, and they in turn would have girl children who love horses."

She laughed at this.

"It is not your blood that has to run in your child's veins," she said, "but your spirit. Ordinary men and women beget life by combining their seed. They abandon themselves and then their children. Every day babies are left alone in the cold to cry and die. The girls of Siberia do not beget—they save lives and give life."

Tankiasis had not understood what I meant.

"But I want to make children in women's hearts," I insisted. "I want to inseminate all the women who put down the burden of their existence and become warriors!"

"You dream too much, Talestria," she said with an indulgent smile. "One day you will meet the girl child destined for you, and she will be your heir."

I had never confided in Tania about these torments. Just like her mother Tankiasis, Tania loved me but did not understand me.

I let my dreams gambol over the steppe and spread through the sky. They were my flocks, and I let them graze among the stars.

. . .

IN OUR TRIBE when a warrior was struck down with the incurable illness of old age, she rode out of the encampment and set off across the steppe without a backward glance. She stopped when she came to a river, lay down in the grass, and let the predators and scavengers devour her.

Tankiasis followed these ancestral directives. She had raised me, and now she left. The elders covered up her departure, telling Tania and myself that she had gone to collect weapons from the whale hunters. When her horse returned, I understood the real reason she had gone, and galloped across the steppe for three days in the hopes of finding her.

Tankiasis had vanished. The tall grass undulated, revealing a bird's nest, a stream, a pile of stones marked with dragon's footsteps. The God of Ice had given me a mother and wanted to take her back from me. I challenged his power, resuscitating Tankiasis, who now galloped across the internal steppes of my mind. She had become immortal by my wish, and now she watched over me tenderly and sang to me:

The evil done to you is a force for good.
The good done to you could be evil.
Reacting to evil turns it to the good.
Reacting to good turns it to evil.

You are not indestructible.
You are destructible if you persist in seeing good in evil.
Wonderful things will happen.
You must neither close your eyes nor block your ears.

My mother, Queen Talaxia, had told me that the words of our tribe contained magic. They could make the invisible appear in the visible and transform legend into reality. Tania and I had begun writing a book in secret: at night, lying in the grass, I read the stars and dictated the story of Alestries to her. Tania believed the stars were whispering in my ear, when in fact I found the words already sown in my heart.

Alestries was a little girl who was abandoned and brought up by wild horses. A goddess took her into her celestial meadows and taught her to wield two sabers. At twenty she left the clouds and returned to earth to do battle with monsters. Astride her white mare she knocked at the door of dark shadowy kingdoms and released women chained in palace dungeons. She seduced princesses dying of boredom, dethroned grasping kings, and drove out evil spirits, which metamorphosed into panthers, snakes, birds, and beautiful women with ample bosoms and rounded bellies.

This book writing was interrupted by an alarm signal: a frontier guard to the southeast had lit her beacon. Columns of smoke, relayed by other beacons, spelled out this message: a troop of thirty armed nomads was riding toward us. I asked Tania to lock our book away in a cave, and I raised an army of thirty girls. We galloped for three days to confront the invaders, and a band of tall warriors covered in armor appeared on the horizon. We put on our metal-plated wooden helmets and launched a hail of arrows at them.

. . .

A WOMAN ON a huge white horse rode at the head of the warriors. Long scarlet feathers bobbed furiously on top of her helmet. She looked over my army, and her eyes came to rest on me. My head swam—she had singled me out. Casting aside our arrows with her shield and lance, she bore down on me, and I rode on to meet her despite the knots of emotion in my stomach. Our weapons met, sending out sparks. The point of her lance slid over my shoulder, and I shuddered with pleasure. With one hand I swung my bludgeon at her chest while I twisted my sickle through the air. She spun her horse round, driving back the bludgeon with her lance while my sickle cleaved her shield apart. Her horse leaped and charged again. The warrior woman had unsheathed her sword and swiped the feathers from my helmet.

But I knew this nomad woman!

I drew right up to her to cave her head in; she pushed me back to slit my throat. I opened my arms wide to threaten her; she lunged her lance and drove in her sword; I threw myself forward, she withdrew; I withdrew, she advanced. She hurled herself at me with both weapons drawn like an eagle's steely talons. I fell backward, twisting my sickle around her sword and jabbing her lance with my bludgeon. The sky and our weapons spun in confusion, and in the flashing of those blades her eyes shone, sometimes with fury, sometimes with a smile.

Who are you? Are you that little girl with lily-white skin who ran through the market stalls with me and who was enslaved by the leopard hunters? Are you the little girl with green eyes who shared her gourd of milk with me for one whole summer?

The warrior seemed to hear the questions buzzing inside my head. Her iridescent eyes communicated gusts of unspoken words to me, and those words homed in on the wound on my breast, hurting me.

I sat back up and struck out again. She pushed my arms apart with hers, and our wrists touched. "If you love me," I told her inside my head, "put down your weapons!"

Our labored breath mingled, our pulses raced in time, sweat gleamed on our brows and formed beads on our cheeks.

"Lower your weapons, love me!" I ordered her, still in my head.

She moved quickly.

"No." She rebelled.

My bludgeon broke her lance. Her sword struck my breast-plate, which roared loudly. The earth was trembling, the sky breaking open. I was overwhelmed with joy: She's mine! She will be wild with love for me!

I feigned weakness, inciting her to follow me and drawing her away from her tribe. I escaped Tania, who watched over me jealously, and we rode for days on end, the warrior woman never letting me out of her sight. She followed me, her desire roaring within her, the constant thud of her horse's hooves in the grass, an echo of her body's impatience. The birds flying up in front of my horse, the grass bending aside to let us pass, the clouds drawing closer to protect us from the sun . . . everything sang in chorus: Talestria! I am coming with you. I am yours!

One night as I lay in the grass I heard her voice, deep and rich, rising slowly in the air and wrapping itself around me. With that song in a strange language she communicated to me her loneliness, her melancholy, her quest for a companion in war, on horseback, and in embraces that drive away the wind, the snow, and the cut of a sword. Gazing at the stars, I too began to sing. My song had no words; I followed the intonations of her voice and improvised a tune that made her song stronger and more lovely. Our voices rose, and with them, my soul flew up to the stars. This is Alestries, whispered the ether; this is the heroine who took up residence in your heart before you even met her.

A gentle warmth spread through me: Alestries was not an illusion, she alone was capable of following me in full gallop, in flight, at the speed of light. She alone could slip into my life by way of the stars. I stopped singing and wept in silence. I, the vengeful little girl, the orphan who had crossed the steppes to become an Amazon, I who rested from bloody battles by taking refuge in the legend of Alestries, had just received happiness I was not even seeking: a warrior woman had come to join her sorrow and hope to my own.

I would lose her! Like Salimba, Talaxia, and Tankiasis, like the little girls I had become attached to, like the tribes that had adopted me, she too would disappear and die. Beauty is short-lived on the steppes. The lives I grasped became shooting stars, leaving only darkness in their wake. I dried my tears and curled myself up tightly. As I slept, I heard Tankiasis singing: *You are destructible if you persist in seeing good in evil. Reacting to evil turns it to the good. Reacting to good turns it to evil.*

• • •

DAWN BROKE, AND with it came strength. What of the suffering of separation, what of the pain afforded when the beloved is pierced by arrows . . . I was determined to be joined with Alestries and to experience with her all the madness of our meeting.

But Alestries was a man! I fled—saddened, furious, and in despair—and would have galloped all the way to the ocean had I not been stopped by a river. To us a river is God's revelation: my god had decided to put me to the test, for the greatest good comes from the greatest evil. I was meant to love Alestries despite his body, I was meant to abandon myself to him without counting the time we were granted. Loving is more difficult than waging war: loving is fighting the past and secrets, and everything impossible.

The bolt of light was more dazzling than summer lightning when it struck me, making me tremble to the very tips of my fingers. It knocked the breath out of me, leaving me struggling to compose myself on the inside. Any woman would have been burned out by the flames of a female warrior soul in a man's body. I loved it even more for the suffering it inflicted on me because Talestria, queen of the Amazons, draws strength from pain, making her light shine still brighter, red on the outside and yellow in the center.

Countless men had been decapitated before they could even touch me. This man Alestries was not afraid of me; he held me to him, his hands caressed me to my very marrow, and mine made him moan. The two of us loved each other over and over again until we could no longer see or hear, until his seed mingled with my blood and my seed spilled inside his head.

I was naked; he cannot have failed to notice the scars over my body. He touched the wound deep in the flesh of my left breast, and I sat up with a start. He caught me by the leg and pushed me to the ground, pinning me down by leaping on top of me.

Alestries made a long declaration of which I understood not a single word, but the name Alexander came back again and again. A terrible apprehension chilled my limbs.

"Are you Alexander?" I asked in Persian.

His face lit up; he spoke Persian too. His voice sounded even more solemn in that language.

"We do not know each other," he was saying. "But we have always known each other. There is no point wasting time, all the years spent without you were wasted. No seductions, I hate seductions. No oaths, I hate oaths that are so easily broken. No ceremonies, I have held too many ceremonies. No speeches, I despise the speeches I have given. Nothing official. There is no one here, no one watching us. I give myself to you. You are mine. Alestria, my kingdom is yours. It is proof of my love."

I looked away, uttering not a sound. I wanted to reject him and flee. I had known only treachery and violence from men. Alexander's declaration hurt me: he was lying!

This warrior who had subjugated the world by strength could not know anything of love. He wanted to show off the queen of the Amazons as his proudest trophy on his horse's rump. He was not Alestries, I was wrong. I was about to get up, to gallop off, to exile myself far from him, far from his conquered lands . . . when he rested his head on my heart. His silence pierced right into me and filled me with joy and sadness. His calloused hands stroked my wounds. He kissed me. I faltered, and regretted giving myself to him the previous day as my arms disobeyed me, my mouth reached for his, and my thighs wrapped around him.

"I have searched all over the world," he said in my ear. "Be my wife."

I gave a hoarse involuntary sound:

"Why me?"

"Because everything was written here," he said, stroking the crook of my left breast.

Marrying a man, handing herself over with lowered arms . . . would be a defeat for the queen of the Amazons, who had never been beaten.

"Alexander and Alestria." He spoke our names gently. "We shall conquer the world and join the sun."

The sun!

I, the queen of birds, horses, and grasshoppers, I have people waiting for me: Tania, my sisters, aunts, and girl children. I carry within me the curse of the Amazons, which forbids me to love a man. Marrying Alexander means leaving Siberia, abandoning my kingdom, fleeing with him like every other Amazon in the past who has fallen for a man.

"Come, Alestria! we shall climb mountains and take citadels by storm. We shall fight dragons and monkeys and elephants driven by warriors covered in pearls and diamonds. Be my queen, Alestria. I offer you magnificent lands, thousands of starlit nights, riding alongside one hundred thousand men beneath the sun, in water and sand, through forests and deserts."

Alexander's voice shook me, and I felt I was waking from a long sleep. God had just spoken to me through his words. I should no longer take my revenge on men, I should love the sun! I should lay down my weapons and gallop alongside Alestries!

Alexander's scars rubbed against my own. The man who

wanted to conquer the queen of the Amazons held me in his arms, and I had nowhere to hide. He forged himself a path in my belly, worked his way up my blood vessels, found my heart, and broke the wound that acted as my shield. He found his way onto my internal steppes, where Talaxia, Tanikiasis, and Salimba lived along with all the other beauties who had grown immortal through the force of my memory.

Darius, the king of the Persians, had offered me cloth, palaces, mountains, and precious gems. I preferred the wind, storms, blood, and victory promised by Alexander.

For that, for him, I must die and live again!

"Come, Alestria, it shall be for life and for death," he said.

How could he read inside my head? A burning torrent made my legs weightless, flowed through my chest, and spread down my arms. A beam of light struck my head and burst inside my body, transforming itself into the Milky Way. I have no more questions. Alexander has defeated me. I am his.

Fly, birds, fly to the skies! Alestries and Alestria are setting off for the clouds. We shall conquer the world. We shall fertilize its vastness, filling it with the purity of the glacier and the strength of fire.

Fly, birds! Beat your wings, do not look back at the bushes you have left. Do not go back to your nests. Beat your wings, brave the wind, look to the sun. Look at that red, yellow, and orange, that fusion of ice and flames.

Fly, birds! Fly ahead of all birds, you who love the ecstasy of freedom above all else!

CHAPTER 7

Bucephalus darted in and out of the green waves, opening up a route through the ocean. Accompanied by the chestnut mare and followed by birds of the steppes, he leaped, flicking his hocks and launching himself into the air. Alestria held my reins and rested her head against my chest.

Blue and orange butterflies, purple-winged grasshoppers, and seven-spotted ladybugs flitted over my cheeks and flew away. Rays of sunlight filtered by the clouds were like golden pillars holding up the sky.

I had lost the lust for battle but, in meeting Alestria, had found it again. My troops, demoralized after eight years of campaigns, would find new motivation now they had a queen who was the embodiment of Athena.

Alestria, warrior woman with two weapons, the bludgeon you wield has shattered the hopes of every woman who schemed to become my wife; your sickle has cleaved the heads of every conspirator who wanted me to die alone or in the poisoned existence of an arranged marriage. By freeing me from worrying matrimony, you have freed my strength.

I was ridiculed as a conqueror because I had no queen; my resonant name elicited as much pity as admiration. Watching me return with my most precious conquest, some would be saddened to see me so happy. All those gleefully pointing out that greatness casts a long shadow and glory requires sacrifice would plead with their gods, asking them why they should be deprived of power and beauty, why Alexander should be granted every gift including a woman's love. These men and women whose eyes were always trained on my golden laurel wreath would have to bite their forked tongues; their slander would fly away. They would say Alexander had captured a little savage and claim he was mad to make some rootless girl queen of the universe. They would say he was bewitched by a black-eyed sorceress, and would urge his soldiers to revolt.

But Alexander and Alestria would fly above their malicious gossip, paying no attention to rumors spread by the jealous. They would be king and queen like two stars on a starless night, lighting the earth with their flames. And Alexander's soldiers who so thirsted for light would forget their sorrows and nostalgia, drawing strength from this union of two warriors in order to do battle to the very edge of the universe.

As we rode Bucephalus, I thought of what strategy I would use to introduce my wife to the Macedonian nobility, Greek sophists, Persian viceroys, and barbarian tribal chiefs. I would use cunning to assert her over my empire as I had asserted myself in Macedonia.

I could already hear myself holding forth to my troops:

"Soldiers! Your king has returned accompanied by your queen! Alexander shall march at the head of the army, and Alestria shall bring up the rear and tend to the injured. She shall listen to your wailing and encourage you to overcome pain.

"Soldiers! Your queen is afraid of neither suffering nor death. She challenges the powerful, the rebellious, and the undefeated. She is indefatigable! Be as she is, be better than she is! Be more courageous than a woman; you must not disappoint your warrior queen!"

. . .

I WAS NO longer Talestria. I rested my head against Alexander's chest and listened to his breathing, absorbing his strength and giving him mine. He and I, together: nothing would be impossible.

What reactions would I now face? Who would be the men who welcomed me and the women who busied themselves around me? Alexander was silent, but I could hear the beating of his anxious heart. He was about to make room for me in a life where there was no room for a woman.

Do not worry, I told him in my thoughts. Alestria is not an ordinary woman who has not lived: she is an invincible warrior. She is also the anonymous little girl who has never been afraid of the unknown. I shall respect strange customs and incomprehensible languages. I shall slide into a new world as if it were a new family, learning all its rules and coming to know every member. I shall give the women my support and slaves their freedom. I shall share my joys and keep my sorrows to myself. The greatest army

under the skies will not overawe me; proud and brutal commanders will not make me lower my eyes in submission. I shall live for
you. I shall die with you.

Fly, my bird, my love, my sun, fly toward our fate, toward
our conquest.

You alone will be my enemy, you alone will have the power to
wound me and make me suffer.

•   •   •

A DARK SHAPE appeared on the horizon, then a second. My heart
skipped a beat. Alexander the Great and Talestria were riding together on a white stallion, followed by the chestnut mare. Talestria was held prisoner by the invincible warrior! I dared not move;
not one of the Amazons dared to ready her bow, all frozen in
terror. Not far from us Alexander's soldiers seemed to be in the
same state of stupefaction. Not one of them raised his weapon.

The silhouettes drew closer, and all at once I realized that
Talestria was in Alexander's arms, but her hands were not tied.
She was resting her head against the warrior's chest, and he held
her close to him. She was holding his horse's reins! She was smiling! She looked radiant! My head reeled. A curse had just fallen
on our tribe: my queen was in love!

Both armies held their breath, paralyzed by the sight of their
leaders approaching. Alexander's eye swept authoritatively over
the stupefied crowd, addressing not a single word to his men.
My queen gave no orders. They continued to draw closer, still together, and stepped into the gap formed by the two armies so that
we—the Amazons and Alexander's soldiers—had to follow the
queen and the king. I, Tania, followed Talestria toward the south,

then toward the east, where a huge encampment stood out against the pale sky. Its gates opened: we entered the kingdom of men.

Warriors in short skirts, wrestlers in scarlet leggings, and men in blue and yellow turbans milled between the tents. Women with white, black, or pink skin strolled about with their mixed-race children. Persian merchants prowled up and down, singing the praises of their wares. Aviaries, cages of tigers, and chained leopards were loaded onto carts, waiting for the order to leave. Monsters four times the size of horses, with snouts as long as a boa and ears as wide as a crane's wingspan, filed past, making the ground shudder.

Some women brought us a feast to eat, and a group of men with no hair came to play musical instruments. Slave women arrived with basins, pails of water, and clean clothes. They wanted to undress me, but I grew angry and threw them out of my tent. I sent round orders not to reveal our identity.

I waited anxiously for Talestria, and it was three days before she reappeared, draped in necklaces and rings of gold, her eyes emphasized with blue lines and her head covered with a veil. I greeted my queen with one knee to the ground to demonstrate my sadness and indignation. She sent the slaves away with a wave of her hand, came into my tent, and let down the door.

She threw off her veil with its feather trimming, took off her jewels, and flung them to the four corners of the tent. She tore off her embroidered tunic and asked for pails of water to wash herself. I too disliked the heady Persian perfumes that made her body unrecognizable, and I was quick to pour the water and wash her from head to foot.

"You're angry," the queen said.

"Tania is your serving woman. A serving woman never disobeys her queen."

"I know you resent me," she went on. "Tania, the God of Ice has revealed my path to me: I am not the queen of the Amazons; I shall marry Alexander, but not out of weakness—this is my destiny."

Her words cut me to the core. I clenched my teeth and held back my tears.

"The tribe cannot survive without a leader," she said. "I appoint you as regent and entrust to you the task of finding my heir. Go back to the land of Siberia, Tania. I know your character; you will be unhappy if you stay here."

"Talestria, the indomitable queen of the Amazons, is captive to her own love for a man," I cried, raising my voice. "If this is not of weakness, then it must be a spell! Tell me Alexander made you drink a magic potion! Admit that he stole your soul and locked it in some evil casket! Wake up, Talestria! The Amazon queens of the past entrusted you with the tribe's survival. You cannot abandon us!"

"I shall never forget them. I shall never forget you."

Tears flowed over my queen's cheeks, but her voice remained steady.

"The queens were wrong. I am not Talestria: she should have been you. Be strong, Tania, be the invincible warrior woman who fears no separation and who does not suffer when she loses a sister. Go back to our country. You must teach the language of birds to the girl children who will be our heirs."

"My queen," I said, beginning to sob, "you have forgotten the warnings of our ancestors! The Great Queen loved a man, she died for him, and the mountain was covered in snow for all eternity."

"I have forgotten nothing," she said, and although her eyes shone, her calm demeanor chilled me to the bone. "I have forgotten nothing. I am not afraid of being cursed. I have faith in my god!"

I spilled a great torrent of tears: my queen was under Alexander's spell. Her life was in danger. How could I leave her?

"So long as you are alive I will not be regent. That is the ancestral rule; there is no point insisting. I shall follow you to the ends of the earth, I shall not go back to our country."

I wept more and more copiously, and the queen, abandoning her reserve, wept with me. The night wore on, and she eventually fell asleep next to me . . . or perhaps she feigned sleep, as I did.

Disgust, disappointment, and anger alternated with tenderness and regret. Like the Great Queen, Talestria was in love with a man: this meant the end for our tribe; our race was condemned to disappear, such was our fate. How was I, Tania, to whom Talestria had offered her braid and her power, how was I to stop the inexorable extinction of a tribe about to lose its queen? Talestria was asking me to cheat the prophecy: to go back to our country and announce that she had died in battle.

How could I appease the anger of our god by hiding the truth? How could I tear myself away from Talestria, the queen of my heart, the sister I had watched over with all my vigilance, the one person my body and soul would fly to wherever I might be? How could I capitulate before Alexander without a fight? Without me, she would drown in an ocean of baubles and precious metals, things that could be bought and sold, and she would wither and fade in a corrupt world where people's faces were distorted with greed, a world where they put birds in cages. My queen had betrayed the tribe. I, Tania, was responsible for this wrong: I had to exile myself with her, to die with her.

I remembered happier times when we lay in the grass and the queen dictated the story written in the stars. I wrote her words down by candlelight and let them transport me to a magic world. The ink I used dried and turned white. But Alexander's arrival had interrupted this writing; we had to pack our things away hastily and set off at a gallop.

I wept and wept and wept again. I remembered Talestria fighting an unknown warrior, both of them crossing weapons, hurtling toward the horizon and disappearing. When they reappeared on the steppe, we no longer had a land or any ancestors. We will never see the white cranes with crimson heads again; we will no longer be called the girls who love horses.

The following morning the queen called the twenty-nine warrior women together in my tent. I, Tania, her scribe and spokeswoman, announced Talestria's decision and said:

"I, Tania, who have acted as her scribe, shall be the firefly lighting her way right to the land of the dead. Who among you will take my braids and become regent?"

Sitting around me in a semicircle, they began to sob. Not one of them wanted to be regent. Not one of them wanted to tell the tribe that Talestria and Tania had died in battle. Not one of them had the courage to lie or to tell the accursed truth: the queen was in love with a man and had run away with him. Not one of them wanted to be the one to go back to our country and announce the arrival of snow for all eternity. They all swore to keep the secret of our origins and to renounce our past.

When a wound will not heal, we amputate the limb it is on. So that no one might know our secret—that the Amazons no longer had a queen—we removed the letter *T* from our names. We lost our family and our freedom. By choosing to be loyal to the queen, we became nameless birds in Alexander's aviary.

I turned and glared furiously at Alestria, but she was staring impassively into space.

Alestria, wake up!

Alexander, torturer of the Amazons, I hate you not only in this life but into the next!

. . .

WHEN HE SAW me coming back to the encampment with a woman on Bucephalus, surrounded by a crowd prostrating itself to welcome me, Bagoas went mad. He sprang up and ran to my tent, screaming. He ransacked my furniture and stabbed a slave who tried to stop him. Then he clawed at his own face and rolled on the ground, beating his chest with his fists. The Macedonian generals lowered their heads, the Persian military commanders looked away, women covered their children's eyes and withdrew. Hephaestion and his guards managed to catch the ranting Bagoas and administer a substantial dose of a drug to calm him. That night silence reigned: not a murmur, not one clink of armor. My generals sat in painful, silent indignation. My soldiers wondered what lay in store for the empire.

But I had made my decision, and no one could sway me. Neither the Persians' amazement nor the Macedonians' anger, neither Bagoas's screaming nor Hephaestion's reasoning, could make me change my mind: Alestria would be my queen.

I summoned Oxyartes, the satrap of Bactria, and ordered him to recognize Alestria as one of his daughters. I chose the Persian name Roxana, "resplendent one," for my future wife.

Our marriage saw sumptuous celebrations in every conquered city in the Orient and right through to the West. Every people had to celebrate the union of Alexander the Great with an Asian woman, a symbolic gesture from the king who encouraged them all to follow his example.

The celebrations in our encampment proved lackluster: the singing was far from exalted and the dancing listless. Cassander did not attend the banquet; neither did Bagoas, who had a fever and was unable to leave his bed. The Persian satraps came to touch the tips of my golden shoes and kiss the hem of the queen's robes, then slipped away into the night. The Macedonian generals renewed their vows of loyalty to me, but their droning voices betrayed their disappointment: they would have liked a Macedonian queen who could have produced a prince with brown hair and green eyes. They would have liked one of their own to have found a way to temper her husband's ambitions, slow his headlong journey east and take his troops back west.

I let my eye rove over the shadows lit with firelight. Ox and mutton turned on spits, silhouettes spun in and out of the sparks. Alestria sat in pride of place beside me, wearing a crimson robe embroidered with three phoenixes in gold and silver thread, and stitched with precious stones. Her cheeks were painted and her eyes made up in Persian style. Her dark eyes shone as she viewed this gathering of dignitaries and drunken soldiers with pride and indulgence. I slipped my hand discreetly under her veil trimmed with gold bells and found hers. Our fingers sought each other and linked together, whispering to each other and silencing the hubbub of the outside world.

I communicated my distress to Alestria: it was a long time since I had shared the same vision as the Macedonians. My own people thought of deserting the battlefields and returning to their native land even more than the Greeks and Persians. They had not fallen for the exotic fruit or spiced food, the fragrant orchids and soft tunics or the solid shoes that were so much more hygienic. They felt they had fought long enough and accumulated enough wealth. The lure of all the comforts they could now afford weakened their resolve: they no longer wanted to die, they did not want to suffer anymore.

Her hand stroked mine and replied: I shall suffer for you. I shall die for you. I shall follow you to the ends of the earth. Keep advancing toward the sun, do not stop.

How can I send the Macedonians away? I cried without words. They chose me when I was a young king with no glory. They bear the memories of terrible battles on their lacerated skin. They supported me in my rise to power, and fought for my title as King of Asia. Without them I would be simply Alexander, son of Philip.

Do not look to your past, she replied; turn to the future. You are Alexander, and you are also Alestria. Everything that is beautiful in my body and soul, everything that I have lived, the vastness of my native land, the blessings of my millennial ancestors . . . all these are yours. Enriched by Alestria, you are the most powerful man on earth. I am the happiest woman under the heavens. We shall set out alone, side by side, without armies or slaves, to meet the sun.

I squeezed her hand hard, feeling its rough skin and calluses, its strength and determination—a hand so like my own.

A band of guards suddenly appeared, cutting through the crowd to tell us a group of foreigners had arrived and wanted to present the queen with a gift in private. It was a huge gold-painted box, and I asked for it to be delivered to my tent. Inside it lay a man with delicate features, wearing a blue turban adorned with golden leaves. It was Darius, already dead, a gold-handled dagger in his left breast. His face was drained of blood but artfully made up; his eyes were half closed, and he seemed to be smiling.

One of the men veiled from head to foot presented Alestria with a clay tablet. She inhaled sharply, and I asked her to read the signs engraved on the tablet.

You have the truth.
You have the freedom to love.
You have the freedom to choose.
To choose is to love.

I did not call for Bagoas to confirm the identity of the body; it no longer mattered to me whether Darius was dead or alive. Let him be buried in secret with the honor and ceremony that befits his rank. His poem was intended for me: Alestria had chosen me, I no longer had a rival.

The campfires went out, and dawn broke.

Outside my nuptial tent soldiers busied themselves and horses champed impatiently. I leaped to my feet and eased on my battle dress.

Alestria, I entrust you with my encampment, which will now

be called the Queen's City. I leave you the women and children, the laborers and vendors and the ten thousand guards. I am advancing into battle, and you will join me later.

Alestria, my queen, do not cry. We shall see each other in thirty days. Your god will protect me from the arrows of the enemies to my front, and my god will stop the lances thrown by conspirators to my rear. Wait for me, my little rain swallow, my red laurel. I shall return to shower your body with my seed. Our love will come to life, and that life will outlast all the seasons of eternity.

I lifted the door of the tent, and my eunuchs fell to their knees and prostrated themselves on both sides of the red carpet that led to Bucephalus. I jumped into the saddle and turned round one last time.

Alestria was standing outside the tent. She looked so small, weeping in the wind, and the sight of her pained me. She ran over to me, barefoot. To fight the urge to take her in my arms, I turned Bucephalus and kicked him straight into a gallop.

Our horses jostled, our lances clashed, barked orders rang in the air. The barbarian horns announced our departure for a still more difficult war. The morning sun devoured me, and my dazzled eyes saw that succession of armies and cities and peoples. I had freed myself from them to marry a queen without a kingdom. Now I had to tear myself from her to fight other armies and conquer other cities.

Such was my fate.

•   •   •

A HOT SPRING ran through a meadow, and there, sheltered from men's eyes, women bathed, rubbing each other's backs, combing each other's hair, and lying on the banks dotted with flowers I had never seen before. A Persian woman told me they were called orchids: they waved their slender leaves at me and watched me with their petal-eyes. They fussed and hid behind each other, jostling and whispering together. Alestria sat on a flat stone, sadly gazing at her reflection while her serving women poured water over her with golden ladles, and cooled her limbs with fragrant mint leaves.

I knew she was still thinking of Alexander. When she looked at herself in the water, it was him she saw. My queen's sorrow made me suffer, and to distract her, I made a little boat drawn by butterflies. Sitting on its prow, she smiled at last and I, Ania, took up the oars and followed the flow of the source, singing:

Butterflies are our sisters.
Because they too love flowers.
With their frail wings they can fly over mountaintops.
They flutter among the clouds for days without food.
We, the daughters of Siberia,
We, the daughters of Siberia,
Our bodies are just as robust,
Our wings just as fragile.

A butterfly with broken wings turns into a dead leaf.
An Amazon with broken wings turns into a lost soul.
A butterfly with broken wings turns into a dead leaf.
An Amazon with broken wings turns into a lost soul.

Alestria turned a deaf ear as she gazed aimlessly and smiled stupidly at the clouds.

I led her over to an anthill.

"Look at the way they go forward, retreat, turn round, and set off again. Ants have no eyes; they respond only to their queen's thoughts. She hides in her underground palace, directing all of them, just as a soul coordinates the limbs of the body it inhabits. Without their queen ants have no sense of direction, they dare not go out for fear of not finding their way home. They wander through the underground tunnels, getting cold and hungry. If attacked they are incapable of defending themselves and die one after the other."

Alestria said nothing; she was not listening to me. Alexander had taken her ears with him so that he could whisper his incantations of love to her and keep his spell over her from afar.

I dragged Alestria by the hand and showed her some bees gathering pollen from flowers.

"I hate bees!" I cried. "They're thieves and assassins! Drawn by the flower's fragrance, they dance round it, singing it songs and swearing their undying devotion to it. The flower naively opens its petals and welcomes the bee into its heart. The bee kisses the flower until it finds the nectar, but once it has, it flies away. The flower, now pregnant to the bee, bears its fruit and dies of sorrow."

Still Alestria said nothing, and tears came to my eyes. I caught a grasshopper and spoke to it:

"You who are so small and so swift, you who travel the earth so tirelessly, be my messenger! Climb mountains, follow rivers, fly toward the steppes! Fly to the land of Siberia! From flower to leaf, from leaf to branch, from stone to tree . . . one morning you will leap into the open hand of one of our sisters! Tell her we are not dead, we will come back, the queen is well and thinking of her sisters. Then, grasshopper, do not waste any time, come back quickly to give us news of Siberia. You will tell us: everyone is well back there, the babies have grown and can already run and ride. One of the great-aunts has gone away to die. We were attacked, but we defended ourselves and our queen would be proud of us. Come back, Talestria! Come back, Tania!"

Alestria started to run. I ran after her, crying:

"Wherever Alexander goes, the earth shakes beneath his feet and birds fly away. Where Alexander's army goes, the grass is trampled, flowers cut down, trees uprooted, and rivers filled with bodies. Where there are no paths, Alexander burns down the forests. Where men resist him, he massacres them and carries off their women. You have been blinded, my queen!"

I held back my tears and gave one last scream:

"I hate Alexander!"

My voice was carried by the wind and resonated round the valley for a long time before going to join the clouds. I had never cried so loudly; that one scream set me free. I realized I was no longer afraid of the assassins who had torn me from my mother's breast.

CHAPTER 8

The rain kept falling. Rain mingled with hailstones spattered on the soldiers, who covered their heads with their shields. Violent winds pushed them over, battering them with broken branches. They struggled through the icy mud, looking in vain for some purchase by prodding their lances into the ground. The first row fell backward onto the second, who took all the rest with them. As they fell, they injured themselves on each other's weapons. Their terrified horses whinnied and tried to clamber back to their feet. Lightning tore through the darkness, striking the earth with a terrible crackling and briefly illuminating the trees so that they looked like Titans looming out of the earth. The Persians knelt to pray while the Greeks and Macedonians looked for a means of escape.

Still riding Bucephalus, I forged a route through the chaos. As the thunderclaps covered my men's desperate cries, I shouted at them, forcing them to get back up, to form orderly ranks and advance. The rain blinded me and turned my limbs to ice, rain that wanted to wipe Alexander's army from the face of the earth, rain acting as a messenger for unknown powers that wanted to stop me in my headlong race against myself.

The rain kept falling, weaker but persistent. We had pitched our tents and lit fires when a Persian soldier burst into my tent to report the pitiful state of his regiment, and then himself collapsed. I had him carried to my bed and continued my discussions with my generals. When the poor boy came to, he was startled: ashamed and terrified to find himself sleeping in Alexander's place, he prostrated himself at my feet and begged me to punish him.

"Soldier," I said, "Darius would have condemned you to death for sullying his throne. Alexander asked for you to be carried to his bed in order to save your life. With Darius your life had barely any value; you were an armed slave who could be broken and abandoned. With Alexander you are a free man, a respected warrior. Go back to your regiment and tell them to rest before the next battle."

. . .

THAT RAIN HERALDED painful ordeals. A young page called Hermolaus, the son of a noble Macedonian warrior called Sopolis, was secretly plotting to assassinate me. When his scheme was denounced by one of his accomplices, he was taken before an assembly of Macedonian soldiers because the law of our native land granted them the right to try him and condemn him. The young page acknowledged his crime without shame and used the opportunity to whip up the crowd.

"You, Alexander, have killed innocent people! Attalus, Parmenion, Philotas, Alexander of Lyncestis, and Cleitos all protected you with their shields in the face of enemies; they suffered injuries to guarantee victory and glory for you. But this is how you thanked them: Cleitos drenched your table with his blood, Philotas was tortured and exposed to jeering from the Persians he himself had defeated, you used Parmenion to kill Attalus and then had him assassinated too. That is how you rewarded your Macedonians!"

The soldiers cried out in protest, and Sopolis was tempted to throttle his own son. I calmed them with a firm wave of my hand, and invited Hermolaus to go on.

"We have endured too much of your cruelty as well as the humiliation you inflict on us by making us dress like barbarians! You love living like a Persian, but it is a Macedonian we want to fight for!"

Those names—Parmenion, Philotas, and Cleitos—echoed in my ears like so many thunderclaps. Those who had been father, lover, and friend to me had betrayed me and had all ended up in a bloodbath. But the evil they had sown lived on in men like Hermolaus. Even dead, they were still conspiring, urging soldiers to avenge their alleged innocence.

If Hermolaus were put to death, other conspirators would soon replace him. There would always be discontent, anger, rebellion—they go hand in hand with victory. For Alexander was not unique; there were as many different Alexanders as there were Macedonians, Persians, Greeks, soldiers, women, and children. Every people judged him according to their own culture and religion. Every man understood him according to his upbringing, his parentage, and his past. Those who had already met him judged him on just one word, one look, the color of his skin, what he was wearing, or his mood when they saw him. Those who had never seen him formed an opinion about him from rumors and legends that could inspire admiration or hatred. They all took what they needed from him and rejected him when that harmed their own interests.

Neither Plato nor Aristotle had ever pondered this phenomenon. No man had ever inspired such extreme passions. Loved and feared, desired and loathed, I had capitulated before this extension of myself. From East to West, I offered myself to the living and to those who would curse me or sing my praises after my death. I was their horrifying shade from the tenebrous depths, or a ray of sunlight awakening life and distributing poetry. I was their god and their sacrifice.

. . .

"SOLDIERS OF MACEDONIA, you have voted for Hermolaus to die! He and his accomplices will be stoned. But I have decided to spare members of their families, who, according to our law, should die along with the criminals.

"Alexander responds to violence with clemency! He is not afraid of betrayal, he knows how to live with conspirators, he feels no self-pity for his pain, he still trusts you.

"A king who has not survived betrayal is not a great man, he is not worthy of leading an army. To those who want to deflect me from the path of my fate, to those who want to stop my progress toward the Orient, I say, Show yourselves now! Alexander is waiting for you!

"Hermolaus accuses me of becoming a Persian. How could a Persian talk to you like this in Macedonian?

"What is a Macedonian? He is a man capable of marching for days on end without food or water, and who throws himself at enemies with ten times as many troops. He is a man who kills without batting an eye and who does not weep when his father and brothers fall.

"I am accused of exhausting you and dragging you into endless wars. I am accused of wanting to conquer the world. I am accused of spreading Macedonian glory to the very outposts of humanity. Soldiers, think of those who stayed in our native land and who are watching you! Aging men who envy you because you are marching with the greatest army in the world; children who dream of giving war cries on the battlefield; wives adorned with the gold you have sent them; and mothers weeping with pride when they hear of your victories.

"You, my young, strong, beautiful soldiers, are you already thinking of going home? Are you ready to renounce being masters of the world; would you prefer to go back and plow fields, tend sheep, and die of old age in a bed? Are you not afraid of being called cowards, weaklings, deserters? Are you not afraid to hear people muttering when you walk along the street: That's the man who left Alexander, he's hiding at home while his brothers, with a shield in one fist and a lance in the other, throw themselves at enemy ramparts and die in battle!

"Soldiers of Macedonia, in your footsteps cultures blend together, languages intertwine, children are born with the intelligence of the Jews, the refinement of the Persians, and the vitality of the Macedonians. In a thousand years, in ten thousand years, people will still sing of our magnificent army, and your names will be engraved in all eternity.

"As King of Asia, I lived as a simple soldier, you know that. All that is mine also belongs to you. I am your reason, your every word; you are my acts, my hope, the realization of who I am. My army and I are but one! What I want is what you want too: a path carved out by our weapons, a wide road to the very foot of the sun.

"To achieve this unprecedented conquest we need the help of the Greeks. We also need the Persians whom we defeated by our strength and converted by our ambition. The differences in language, customs, religion, and gods mean nothing. Alexander unites them in this one truth: without him, warriors are merely instruments of death. With him they are a celebration of life!

"Come now, soldiers, repeat after me:

"Weariness is fleeting.

"Nostalgia can be defeated.

"Courage is our strength.

"The Indus River is roaring, calling to us!"

. . .

THE SUN WAS obstructed by trees so vast that seven soldiers with open arms could not encircle them. Their gnarled branches wrapped in lichen and fungus stretched out horizontally, bearing roots that hung down to the ground. Creepers wider than a man's thigh clung round their trunks, entwining them to fill the gaps and reach the skies. We were lost, turning round in circles and coming back to where we had set off. Maps had betrayed us, and trading posts had long since disappeared. Instead of paths there were leaves, round, oval, serrated, shaped like feathers, hands, lances; and flowers, their seeping, gleaming, tufted throats exhaling a sweet, fetid perfume.

My soldiers broke through the vegetation with axes and swords. We all suffered the same discomforts as leeches dropped from the trees and gathered on every patch of bare skin. When we tore one off, another arrived, still more thirsty for blood. Our legs were nicked by venomous thorns, and the swelling and itching spread all over our bodies. We scratched ourselves till we broke the skin. Some soldiers were bitten by snakes and died of sudden fever; others forgot my orders and rushed to drink from ponds, only to succumb to debilitating diarrhea.

Seeing our expedition reduced to endless suffering, I took out a map, traced a straight line all the way to the Indus, and ordered my men to set fire to the trees where they formed impenetrable walls. The flames broke through the trees, and sunlight poured into the forest. Tigers, monkeys, snakes, and clouds of birds fled the columns of smoke. Near-naked men with tattooed faces and piercings in their ears and noses emerged from their hiding places in the luxurious vegetation, brandishing weapons.

Whistling arrows, the screams of men fighting, and the clash of weapons woke me from the torpor of that wearying march. Turning a deaf ear to my advisers, who begged me to keep to the rear, I headed up the Macedonian troops to give my men courage and strength. But the fighting was more difficult here: my troops were used to confrontations in formation and were thrown by these men coming down from the branches, appearing from the undergrowth, and vanishing up rock faces. Their archers clung to creepers and jumped from tree to tree without putting a foot to the ground, and their trained monkeys threw themselves at our soldiers and bit their faces.

On the ninth day our men abandoned their horses, and the enemy no longer needed to take refuge in the trees. The injured fought to the death, and the living, covered in blood, went on slitting each other's throats in appalling hand-to-hand combat. I had lost my helmet, my lance, and my sword but grabbed the king of the savages and we rolled to the ground, his hands squeezing my throat. I saw stars against a dazzling white sky. As I struggled to free myself, I kneed him: my vision cleared and the enemy's hairy fingers released their grip. I gathered the last of my strength, raised myself to my knees, and shattered his skull with a rock I grasped. His hideous face grew bigger and bigger as I hammered at his head, screaming, while his brains oozed over my fingers. His eyes rolled upward, his lips drew back to reveal yellow teeth, and he breathed the unbearable exhalation of death over me.

For three days after that battle I shut myself away in the darkness of my tent and saw no one. I lay inert on my bed, surrounded by dancing flames. The fires of the shades encircled me; yellow flames burned me, blue flames chilled me to the marrow, black flames devoured me, and I ran screaming—there was fire everywhere. A wave of it swept over me, followed by another, and in the middle of those flames were dark, silent, icy corridors. I was burning but I was cold, fleeing while my teeth chattered. Every now and then I remembered I was Alexander, but the flames laughed and growling voices chorused:

You are one of us!

You are one of those warriors we send to the earth
To burn and destroy.

The sun, where is the sun?

Where is Apollo who made me invincible? The flames grimaced at me and danced frenetically while the voices rang out:

Invincible?
This is where you will be destroyed.
This is where you will return.

"I don't want to be destroyed!" I cried out. "I am Alexander! I am the king of all men, let me go!"

But still the flames held me, stifling me. Voices whispered to me, saying there was no escape; I struggled and prayed to Apollo to send me his rays. Suddenly a beam of light pierced the shadows. I clung to it like a ladder, climbing back toward life, only to find I was lying in my tent in total darkness.

Feeling my way, I stood up, then tripped, fell and stood again. I opened the door and saw shapes coming toward me. Thinking they were talking flames, I took a step back. Then my eyesight cleared, and I recognized Hephaestion, Crateros, Cassander, and Bagoas.

"We greet you," they cried respectfully. "We greet you, Alexander, King of Asia, and wish you a long life!"

I came back to my senses under my friends' watchful eyes and surrounded by gleaming weapons.

"Bring me food!" I ordered. "I want to eat this life, to devour it. Bring me drink! I want feasting and drunkenness!"

My eunuchs came running, my pages busied themselves. Soon there were tables laden with fruit, meat, pitchers, and goblets. Generals, commanders, and a whole display of beautiful young men lounged on soft carpets. I took the first young man I liked in my arms, and the heat of his youthful body warmed my limbs that still felt so cold; his kisses made me forget the burning scars. I gave him orders to press mangoes, grapefruit, and pineapple over my face, showering me with the sugar of life as I inhaled the fragrance of nature. For tomorrow, under the ground, the sky will be black forever and there will be no more pleasure.

As I brought the umpteenth goblet to my lips, I remembered I had a wife: I threw down the goblet and called Bucephalus. Despite Bagoas's weeping and exhortations, despite Hephaestion's sad expression, I set off at a gallop with a troop of one hundred soldiers. I traveled for many days, flying across the land, I could not wait to have that feeling once again, the most vibrant feeling of earthly life: holding Alestria in my arms.

I renounced sleep, forcing my soldiers to ride on through the night. I could not wait any longer. Waiting meant risking death itself.

At last I saw the ornate outline of my flags, then a silhouette. Alestria was waiting on horseback at the entrance to the camp. I galloped on, and she kicked her mare toward me. I leaped to the ground and ran over to her; she slipped from her horse's back and ran to me. How long it seemed to take! Let me reach her before the underground fires leap up and take me back to their kingdom! Alestria tripped, then tossed off her golden shoes and tied up the bottom of her tunic. I opened my arms, and she threw her arms around my neck, pressing her weight against me. I carried her all the way to our tent, where I tore off her clothes and undressed myself in a flash. My lips clung to hers, my body found hers. Her cool skin soothed my worries, and her tongue rolling over my cheeks and my chest put out the shadowy fires.

Bear me a child, Alestria! This child will be proof of our union and will have the purity I have lost. This child from your belly will wipe clean the horrors sown by Alexander. I am not worthy to be king. He shall be, though. He will be transparent as the glacier and ardent as a mountain on fire. He will have my dignity and your magic, the innocence of a girl married to the power of a warrior king.

. . .

I DID NOT wait for daybreak before setting off on my return journey. I left behind the tears of my queen. I left behind her hair, which smelled of roses and mint. I left behind her wooden comb, her golden hair grips, her body curled up in despair. I galloped to flee my own pain while a voice inside my head screamed that I would never see her again, that that was our last embrace. Tears flowed over my cheeks but were dried by the wind. I urged my horse on to drive away my thoughts: I must carry on with my war.

I rejoined my Macedonian troops, who complained that their legs were lacerated by the undergrowth. They showed me where their arms had been devoured by leeches, hornets, and mosquitoes, and dragged me to where the injured lay dying with gangrenous wounds. Hepahestion, Crateros, and Cassander took turns trying to convince me we must turn back. I clenched my fists and reasoned with them: beyond the forest there were cities more wonderful than Babylon, civilizations more evolved and religions more sublime than any westerner could have imagined. All these wonders had to be ours. The last of my friends withdrew, and Bagoas appeared to talk to me of conspiracies: I listened to him and then sent him away.

Parrots chattered in the trees, and tigers roared in the distance. Then there was silence around the encampment. A rustling sound from deep within the woods wound between the tents, making the campfires flicker before disappearing into the trees.

Having recovered from the initial shock, the barbarian soldiers threw down their weapons and prostrated themselves, crying: "Spirits! spirits!"

Standing outside my tent, I turned away from my soldiers' misery, and stared up at the tops of those dark, shady trees. Alexander would find a way to overcome the conspiracy of men and spirits. The suffering was only short-lived. I must keep on advancing and would never retreat.

．　．　．

HORDES OF SAVAGES plagued us again. Having not mastered the art of molding metal, they used stone daggers and bludgeons made of rocks bound to sticks. They launched wooden arrows dipped in lethal poison. The Persians explained that these hairy-bodied people, the Gonya, were descended from apes. A million years earlier an epidemic had struck the men living in the depths of the forest, and they could no longer couple with their women. To ensure the continuity of the race, the tribes had captured great apes to inseminate their women. The Gonya believed in gods, I learned, but the apes had no religion—that was their difference.

The rainy season was upon us, and storms broke out several times a day. In the rare bright periods the Gonya appeared, wearing coats and hats of sewn banana leaves, to continue with their offensives. They fell into the traps we had dug in the ground and got caught in nets I had strung up between the trees. A succession of strange creatures paraded before me: some extended their own teeth with boar tusks; others had a short bony tail between their buttocks; some were tattooed; others were painted, pierced, or adorned with feathers, amulets, and tiger's tails.

They were interrogated by my Persian interpreters, who spoke so many languages that they understood the Gonyas' speech in a matter of days. After days of marching through the mud they took us to the village of the Boonboongonya tribe, which supplied poison to the entire region.

The village was huddled against a steep rock face and sheltered from the outside world by gigantic trees that acted as pillars for a thick wall of ivy covered in thorny creepers. My soldiers tried to breach this wall, but immediately developed a rash on their hands and arms; they rolled on the ground screaming in pain. Communicating in gestures, one of our guides explained that a labyrinth of seven walls of vegetation protected this ancient tribe, and only its own members and their monkeys knew how to get through it. On my orders, my soldiers camouflaged themselves and watched the comings and goings. In three days they captured dozens of monkeys carrying bamboo tubes full of deadly venom; these were intended for neighboring tribes who gave them *hashna*—the grass of happiness—in exchange. One of the Gonya prisoners told us it was rare to meet a Boonboongonya because they were famed for their laziness.

The monsoon was over, and I forced my way into the village with fire. My troops took cover beneath their shields and finally broke into the kingdom of poisoners, but they encountered no hail of pebbles or lethal arrows. A strange sense of calm reigned over the village, where the only sounds were birdsong and the whisper of a waterfall. Dense shrubs and flowers shaped like water lilies with pistils like red snake's heads wound into an intoxicating labyrinth. I followed the monkeys in secret passageways to reach their masters: a group of Boonboongonya were sunbathing outside their huts, men with matted hair, a tiny tail at the end of their backs, and wearing a seashell to hide their genitals. Some were asleep on the bare earth; others rubbed yellow and black powder into their skin. Seeing us approaching, they smiled to reveal green teeth: they chewed *hashna*, I was told, which made them dream with their eyes open in broad daylight.

All at once we heard piercing cries, and a group of Boonboongonya females appeared, naked save for the red paint that covered them. They threw down handfuls of snakes, millipedes, and pestle-shaped stones. My guards were quick to grab them, but they in turn screamed, watching their hands go purple as they came in contact with the creatures.

The males of this tribe did not work: the women could cast a spell over the monkeys to enlist their help in their work and to climb trees to pick fruit, which was their main source of food. They drugged crocodiles and taught them to chase snakes. They covered their children in a paste made of poisons from plants, centipedes, and spiders; this made their thick hair fall out, leaving smooth skin and unwrinkled faces. When a crocodile brought them a snake, they attached it to an instrument and tortured it until it spat out its most deadly venom. Mixed with black powder and toxic roots and leaves, and pounded by the monkeys, it became the lethal concoction known as *boonboon*.

Like all Gonya peoples, the Boonboongonya lived as a community and had no concept of family. The males did not have a role as fathers, and the females bore children that belonged to the whole tribe. Unlike other Gonya, though, the Boonboongonya had lived a long time in isolation, and their blood had degenerated. The males had grown so lazy they no longer even bothered to mount their females; that was why there were so few young. Those who looked young were in fact old but still had beautiful skin thanks to the poison wraps; those who looked old were over a hundred.

My soldiers were disappointed not to have found an antidote to the deadly poison, as the Boonboongonya did not make one. And they were horrified when, on the night of a full moon, they heard wails so harrowing their skin crawled. The Boonboongonya had congregated near the waterfall and chosen one male and one female from among them. Without any ceremony they tore them limb from limb while they were still alive, grilling hunks of their flesh on the fire, tossing their organs to the crocodiles, and giving the bones to the monkeys to gnaw.

My soldiers slaughtered the cannibals with their lances. Their blood spilled, and when it came in contact with my men's skin, it left red patches that itched terribly. Any unfortunate whose eyes were splattered with this blood lost his sight for several days. I asked for the black and orange millipedes to be released from their containers of woven leaves and ordered that the huts be set alight. The flowers caught fire, and with them instruments of torture, wooden mortars impregnated with poison, and vessels made of bamboo. The bitter smell released by them gave my men migraines.

My army did not even wait till dawn to decamp and flee those nauseous flames. The *boonboon* monkeys ran after us, moaning. One of them leaped at Bucephalus and climbed onto my shoulder, hanging round my neck and not wanting to leave me.

I named it Nicea.

. . .

"THE MACEDONIANS DON'T understand why you have abandoned the sumptuous palaces," Hephaestion told me, "or the hordes of concubines and the constant banqueting, and all for this endless marching across the arid Bactrian mountains onto the Scythians' steppes and into the luxuriant forests of the Indies, where you have to battle with monsoon rains, ape-men, and snakes. They now realize that Alexander seeks neither gold nor glory, and they no longer believe in your constant promise of diamonds. Without the lure of booty, without dazzling victories to flatter their warrior vanity, their every step is weighed down by exhaustion. That is why discontent has spread like an epidemic."

"Hercules tackled the Nemean lion, the Erymanthian boar, and the Cerynian hind," I replied. "He slew the birds on Lake Stymphalus and the Minotaur in Crete, and he put Cerberus in chains. The ape-men are nothing compared to the monsters the hero of yesteryear brought down. Our soldiers will soon see the wealthy cities of the Indies; they will sleep on soft cushions and send home caravans of gold and precious stones."

"The weakness of strength is to believe only in strength," said Hephaestion.

Irritated, I said nothing and sought out Nicea. I had tended and groomed him myself, and the little monkey now had golden fur again and wore a scarlet tunic embroidered with gold thread that I had tailored specially for him. He brought us a tray of fruit, chose the best of the bananas, peeled it carefully, and handed it to me. I smiled.

"Do you know what our soldiers are saying?" Hephaestion went on.

"That the Gonya steep their arrows in poison and the Macedonians in slander," I replied wearily.

"They say you have gone mad!" cried Hephaestion. "They say you have fought too much, galloped too far, and slept too little! Your mind is no longer lucid, hence your stubbornness, your refusal to hear any complaints or listen to advice!"

I made Nicea jump onto my lap.

"Why risk your life fighting creatures that are not even human? Why go on when you have already conquered Persia and been recognized as King of Asia? If you were struck by a poisoned arrow tomorrow, all that glory and the crown would no longer be yours. You, Alexander, do not even have an heir!"

His words hurt me, but I held my temper in check. I opened up a silver casket and showed him the leaves in there.

"Look, Hephaestion, here is the secret of this war: they are *hashna* leaves. They do not grow in this forest, and the Gonya know nothing of cultivating the land. *Men* are supplying them with this mild drug on condition that they make war with us. *Men* are manipulating them to attack us. *Men* are afraid of us and want to drive us out of the Indies before we take their cities by storm and claim their treasures for ourselves."

Hephaestion wanted to reply, but I interrupted him:

"I have been told of a great king called Poros. He is so rich, it is said, that his elephants are covered in precious stones. This gallant warrior dreams of uniting all the kingdoms of the Indies. I have arranged to meet this man, Hephaestion, I must confront him. If I die in combat, you will take our troops back to Persia. If I win the battle, I shall share with you and with all my soldiers the unimaginable treasures of the Orient."

"Are you really so blind? The gods are sending you signs to stop this absurd campaign. The degenerate state of the Gonya proves we have reached the limits of humanity. Beyond this forest there are no more men but the kingdoms of monsters and wild beasts. And do you, the great Alexander, want to lose your soldiers down to the last man in order to be king of those lowly creatures?"

Hephaestion shot a look laden with contempt at Nicea, then withdrew.

Weary of arguing with him, I let him leave. Hephaestion could not understand me: his dream of seeing me venerated as king of the Greeks and Persians had been realized, and any other unexpected dreams were mere poetry and madness to him, a Macedonian nobleman raised by Aristotle like myself.

Two days later in battle an arrow shot from behind drove into the crest of my helmet. Had the soldier's hand wavered? Or had he been ordered to threaten me? Days passed, and still the army could not identify the murderer. I suspected a conspiracy among the highest ranks and entrusted Bagoas with carrying out a secret investigation of my friends' loyalty.

The eunuch reported back all the conversations his men overheard: Hephaestion was angry with me for being so obstinate; Cassander still could not forgive me for marrying an Asian of obscure parentage; Crateros complained that I had grown hard-hearted and said I was deaf; Perdiccas was still mourning the loss of Cleitos, whom I had killed with my own hand; Ptolemy, the eldest and most restrained, was convinced I should be forced to take a year's rest. They all referred to me as the tyrant behind my back.

Shut away in my tent, I taught Nicea how to play a musical instrument. I lay on my bed listening to the monkey plucking the strings of his lute and pictured Alexander, Hephaestion, Cassander, Crateros, Lysimaque, and Perdiccas at school together. At first we had been inseparable, all experiencing our first kisses and embraces at the same time. There were the fits of laughter, the arguments and reconciliations followed by exalted oaths of loyalty. Alexander was right at the middle of that virile little world, playing the capricious girl who knew just how to secure promises and protection.

Those young boys swore they would never leave each other; they decided to conquer the world together. Along the way on our campaigns, carnal love had given way to friendship, and each of us in turn had taken lovers. That band of happy reveling friends had gradually split up as they waged wars and conquered lands. They had all lost their innocence, and I had become an arbitrator, responsible for sharing out glory and wealth: I was both their master and their slave, handing out titles and promotions. They plotted to try to force their ideas on me; they came and begged me to oversee their lovers' upbringing; they formed a united front against anyone who succeeded in getting close to me; they made sure my relationships never lasted long. Their possessiveness grew the farther we marched away from Macedonia. Anything not from our country they condemned as a perversion, a whim, a disloyalty. The Persian clothes and customs I had adopted, the barbarian food I so loved, Bagoas the slave I had given a position, Alestria the Asian orphan I made my queen . . . all were offenses that drove Cleitos to insult me in public. By killing him with my lance, I had broken an oath of eternal friendship.

Nicea abandoned the instrument and turned to massaging my head. The love and gratitude I read in his gaze were not enough to console me. I tore myself from this sadness by turning my thoughts to war.

Withdrawing from the Indies and taking my troops back to Persia would mean giving the Indian princes time to rally around Poros. My soldiers were so haunted by the nightmare of crossing the Indies that—once their minds were relaxed, their bellies fed, and their muscles unwound—they would not have the courage to suffer a second time. Only the ignorant have temerity. To rest was to give up: we had to advance.

Lying in Darius's bed in Babylon, I had laughed at the thought of my victory. Now, in the middle of a hostile forest that featured on no map, I laughed at the thought of my defeat. Losing his friends was a failure for Alexander the Great. Isolated in my tent, betrayed on all sides, I was back to the loneliness of the little boy watching the stars. The pinnacle of my life as a warrior had come full circle. Alone and disarmed, I still had the same dream, though, the same obsession: to conquer beauty.

The headlong gallop toward wonderment knows no limits.

Wonderment is the gold of the sun.

I, Alexander, son of Apollo and Ammon, will not renounce it.

CHAPTER 9

Slaves protected by warriors went ahead of us. Day and night they felled trees and carved out a road on which the Queen's City—a vast nomadic town—could travel through the forest of the Indies in Alexander's footsteps.

At each stopping point the soldiers planted stakes in the ground and built a wall. Ptolemy ruled as master in the men's quarter: he received provisions and gave supplies to the king; he took in the injured sent back from the front, and greeted reinforcements from Greece and conquered lands. Troops were constantly on the move. Over and above the whinnying of horses and the sounding of horns, we could hear the bustle of breeders mating horses from different lands, armorers experimenting with metal alloys, weavers pushing their creaking looms, and cooks noisily slaying calves.

In the women's quarter Alestria rose before the sun to receive

her subjects' salutation: men and women formed a long line outside her tent, and one after the other prostrated themselves at her
feet—all except for the Macedonian warriors, to whom the king
had granted the privilege of greeting her with a bow.

In order to marry her, Alexander had asked Alestria to recognize the satrap Oxyartes as her father and to take the Persian
name Roxana. Being extremely jealous, he required her to wear
a veil in male company. I, Ania, standing beside my queen for
the morning audience, ruminated on my loathing for this man
who had robbed her of her dignity while offering her this daily
spectacle of veneration.

Alestria cast her black eyes over each of her visitors. Military chiefs brought her news from the front; doctors came to
ask for remedies to heal the injured; sages wanted to show her
their inventions; soldiers and their wives told her of conspiracies against the king; madmen, outcasts, and criminals groveled
at her feet; tradesmen, courtesans, and prostitutes lined up to
sing her praises; all of them hoped to reach Alexander through
Alestria, all of them wanted to please the king by flattering the
queen.

The sun followed its course across the sky. The thud of felled
trees, the whicker of foals, and the chanting of slaves wringing
out wet sheets reached the tent. On top of this constant racket,
men came in and argued, women fought and pulled each other's hair while the babies clinging round their necks screamed.
Alestria heard their whispering and sobbing, their shrieked accusations and despairing lamentations, with patience and indifference. People spoke to her in every language: Macedonian,
Greek, Persian, and tribal idiom. She did not understand every-

thing, but they thought she did, confiding in her their concerns and corrosive anger. They came to her so that she could bear their pain, jealousy, and hatred. Alestria accepted these bouquets of venomous flowers without complaining about their vicious thorns, listening to them without uttering a word. Her silence was soothing, her attentive expression a balm on their open wounds, her luminous presence purifying.

Men and women alike left feeling appeased. Alestria was the deep, limpid lake before which Alexander's servants prostrated themselves prior to throwing their waste into it. She said nothing and never spoke to me of it, accepting this earthly waste in silence and transforming it into brilliant red fish, twinkling lights, wafting weeds, and water lilies.

When the sun reached its zenith, the audience came to an end. Once released from her duty, the queen called for her horse, galloped to the entrance to the city, and waited for the king's return, sheltering under a parasol erected for her by the soldiers. She remained motionless, her eyes fixed on the horizon, her body taut as a bow trained toward Alexander, toward the target that did not appear.

If horsemen came into view, her body quivered, preparing to launch into a gallop. But Alexander was not with them; they were bringing her gifts from the king. Sad and disappointed, she went back to her tent. She took a little gold knife he had given her and carefully undid the string, the banana leaves, the leaves of gold and silver, and the petals. A gem, an insect, a box, or a feather would emerge, and she would stroke it and spend the next few days looking at this precious object.

During the audiences her eyes smiled and radiated light. But

I, Ania, her faithful servant, could read through her veil. Her body was there with us, but her soul had flown to those distant lands where Alexander fought. Her body was here, mute and cold, imprisoned by the men and women who needed a queen, while her soul was over there, close to him, where she found her joy, her spontaneity, and her words once more.

Our ancestors were right to forbid love, which turns a woman into the living dead!

Alestria, my queen, had become a stone statue.

· · ·

ALL THE JEWELS he offered me were pebbles.

All that embroidered cloth accumulating in my tent was shrouds.

Nothing was worth as much as his eyes, more precious than emeralds.

Nothing was worth as much as his skin, the most beautiful cloth in the world.

When Alexander realized that these gifts did not dazzle me or comfort me, when he realized that these inanimate things could not replace him, he sent me a parrot, a frog, a girl child covered in hair found on the battlefield.

These creatures that I cared for could not speak for him. In the little girl's eyes I read the terror of someone who has survived a massacre. I gave her the name Alestries, like the heroine of my unfinished novel.

Alestries was starting to walk and could already babble the language of the Amazons. Her accent only heightened my melancholy. Outside it was eternally summer, but in my heart it was winter, endless frost. Alexander was my only springtime, coming round and leaving again.

I did not want to learn Macedonian or Greek; I was not Roxana, Queen of Asia. I belonged to the grasshoppers, the wind, and the pollen, all things that fly away and never come to rest. I was Alestria, who had halted her gallop for a man.

For a man, Alestria had become Roxana. She had renounced the steppe and turned into a flower planted in a silver pot and transported on a golden chariot.

All the tents covered in gold leaf, the warriors bowing at my feet, the beautiful women submitting to me, all the swift horses and the birds with a thousand shimmering feathers—they were all shadows. I wanted only him, his feet, his hands, his breath.

My life was waiting.

My life was worrying.

My life was joy and wrenching pain, endless dozing and awakening.

Was he injured?

Could he find his way?

Had he been struck by a poisoned arrow? Seen the savage leaping at him from the trees?

While I waited, I grew weaker.

I no longer had any appetite for food, games, or pleasure.

I no longer dreamed. I no longer spoke. I was silent.

I did not know what I was waiting for—for him to come back, for him to leave, for his wounded flesh, for his dead body on the top of the pyre.

I forced myself to eat, to get dressed, to arrange my hair. Before Alexander's men and women I hid my despair and forced myself to stand upright, to command and be radiant. I granted each of them a silent blessing, a prayer. Soldiers, wives, courtesans, whores, tradesmen, workmen, slaves, horses, dogs . . . I loved them all because I loved their king.

When alone with Ania, I could not look her in the eye. I was afraid she would discover my secret: I had agreed to be Roxana, Queen of Asia, for the beauty of my beloved. Behind my facade of dignity I had been defeated by suffering, I had grown weak and was no longer worthy of her loyalty. She and the other girls should leave this queen who could not fight her own sorrow. But how could I survive without them?

It was my punishment for relinquishing my freedom.

. . .

I MISSED THE steppe. I missed the calls of migrating birds. I thought of the girl children, the foals, the goats. I missed the smell of our cooking. I missed the song of the steppes. I was no longer Tania, the melancholy girl who liked to savor the pleasures of life in secret. I, Ania, was overrun by the impurities of the world of men, disgusted by their massacres, intriguing, and denunciations. I was tired of living among women who did not know how to enjoy life and who argued all day long over a scrap of fabric, a child's pout, the cost of a ring.

Men and women hovered around me, the queen's serving woman. They threw me compliments, brought me their regional dishes, gave me gifts, and tried to find me a husband. I turned them away with a scowl.

It was so easy to read their thoughts: they wanted to bribe me in order to win the queen's favor. They wanted to know the secret of where we came from, our past, our customs. They wanted to know the queen's moods, what she said, and what she worried about so that they could take great pride in telling the entire city.

These men and women with eyes like an owl's and ears like a dog's started speaking ill of us the moment they were back in their own quarters. The queen's name and the names of her strange servants were on everyone's lips, all these thankless people growing bored while they waited for the king's victory. Rumors circulated from one tent to another: a slave girl, a workman, or a soldier would secretly come to inform me of the latest snippet livening their conversations. I, Ania, listened to this gossip as if suffering a thousand bee stings. In a fury, I stormed into my queen's tent and blurted out the slander I had heard.

People said our queen was an evil witch who had killed Oxyartes' daughter Roxana and had stolen her skin and her identity. They said that the satrap had agreed to play the role of her father in return for command of the army. They said we came from a dark, shady land where women conversed with spirits, that the queen used black magic to ensnare Alexander's heart. They said that I, Ania, was cold and cruel, and that I manipulated the queen. I was the one controlling her and reigning over Alexander through her.

Tears sprang from my eyes and down my cheeks. I threw myself at my queen's feet.

"Let's go home! These people are mad! They are cursed! The warriors of the steppes kill with their weapons, but Alexander's men and women exterminate with their tongues!"

Alestria stroked my hair and told me it was not important. She told me white cranes should be able to fly above the flames.

"Alexander has cast a spell over you! He's hiding behind you to manipulate his people, who need a queen. They want to venerate her, to malign her, to exhaust her!"

"Surely you know I am not Roxana," she said in reply. "What they say about Roxana is of no concern to me."

"You who galloped across the steppe, you who fought the fiercest of men, how can you let these simpletons sully your name? They call you a witch as soon as they have had what they want from you: your goodness and purity. Alestria, let's leave! Leave this evil wasps' nest! Leave Alexander, master of these disloyal men and women!"

"They are disloyal because they are weak. We should pity them. Do not weep."

I could not believe what I had just heard. I was angry with her.

"Do not weep, is that all you can say to me? I weep every day over my queen's fate! Alexander does not love you—he married you to have a child. He wants an heir to guarantee the continuation of his dynasty. Just like Darius, just like the men before him, he wants a son from the queen of the Amazons. That is why he comes back, sleeps with you, then leaves!"

Alestria trembled. My well-aimed words had reached her, cut into her. After a brief silence she said:

"You understand nothing of love, Ania. Love is loved by love."

A dark glow of happiness appeared in my queen's eye. There in the candlelight I saw it overflow, waft past me, and fill the entire tent.

My queen had gone mad.

. . .

ANIA HAD NEVER loved a man. She knew nothing of love or the happiness of reunited lovers: their limbs intertwined, they fell asleep to meet again in their dreams. She did not know the wrenching pain when lovers part, when their bodies feel amputated. She did not know the strength that made me impervious to slander, betrayal, accusations, and intrigues. She did not know this madness: Alexander could take everything from me, I gave myself to him so fully I could tolerate even his absence.

Love lodges itself inside the body, somewhere in the chest. Love does not get lost and cannot be stolen. Love tortured me and made me beautiful. Love made me despair and filled me with hope. I loved Alexander! Those words steeped me in ice-cold water and in flames, brought me joy and pain. They made blue skies and storms. I felt a hundred years old, and I felt defenseless as a child again.

How could rumors have done me harm? How could malicious gossip hurt me? I who stood in the hanging garden of my suffering and my happiness, what did I care for their comments!

I hated the waiting, I loved the waiting! Not being able to touch him, not hearing his voice, made me weep. When I touched him, when I heard his voice, I already thought of how he would tear himself away from me, depriving me of that touch and those words. So I preferred his absence. I went to bed so that I could join him inside my head, on my inner steppes: he kissed me and whispered to me, making me laugh as we rode across the green waves.

Love is tenderness. Love is terror. Love is a soft cushion and a sword against my throat. No longer seeing the one I loved, no longer having to wait for him, never touching him again—that would have severed my very life.

When Alexander got up and put on his armor to go back to war, he would promise me nothing and I would ask for nothing. Warriors know that every day may be the last; they know that to promise is to lie. They prefer death to the cowardice of those who avoid combat. Between Alexander and myself there was only love: the word *death* did not exist. He said nothing to me and I said nothing to him. I helped him dress, fastened his sandals, and arranged his hair with my hands. I touched his curls and breathed in the smell of him. Every time might be the last. Death was there, but we pretended to forget it. We who had come so far, we who had come through seasons, storms, and wars to meet, how could we leave each other?

Oh, the white lily of fear, its dazzling purity and peppery fragrance! That is the offering made by intrepid heroes!

Fear is love's twin. Fear makes love a two-edged sword.

I was afraid from the moment he left in the morning, as his silhouette grew smaller in the distance and was reduced to a trail of dust. I was afraid during the day: a poisoned arrow would burrow into his shoulder, a snake would slither under his armor. I was afraid at night when the howls of famished animals echoed through the woods. I was afraid of traitors and rebels.

Who could say whether we would meet in another life? My god remained silent, and what human would dare make such a promise when every mortal's promise is a lie?

I had lost everything: my weapons, my armor, my helmet. Now that we no longer galloped across the steppes, my horse was wasting away. Ania had grown aggressive, flying into rages, taking refuge in silence, always restless, running off in tears only to return with a stream of accusations. Forgive me, my sister, I would say, leave me here and set yourself free.

I had lost my white cranes, and lost my stars. Now I had nothing but love, that feeble flame on a vast plain shrouded in darkness. I had only that fire to talk to me, to warm me and support me as I struggled with the shadows and battled my fear.

The lily burns like fire. White blends into red. Fear is love. That was all that was left to me, all I had, all that kept me waiting, my life of love in which there was no room for regret.

Alexander was back! He threw down his arms, took off his clothes, and without a word, bore me off to his bed. His skin burned, his muscles still smelled of the tensions of a man who had endured many days' battle. New scars had come to hide the old. He was bleeding. Alexander had changed: I could read pain, determination, and anger in his face. I was riveted by his expression. Bloodied horses leaped from his eyes, hordes of savages with barely any clothes dropped from the trees and threw themselves on me. Alexander crushed my breasts and pummeled my stomach, hurting me. I could not breathe and kept my eyes wide open to tell him that it was me, Alestria, his beloved, whom he was assaulting in this way. Suddenly, as if waking from a nightmare, he froze, studied me attentively, and covered my eyes with his hand. His muscles relaxed, and his free hand stroked me gently, in spite of the calluses and wounds. Our bodies twisted and coiled under the sheets, our sweat mingled. Our breathing no longer told a tale of war but of a long and happy journey in which we would never have to part.

"Don't reject me, Alestria," he whispered. "Keep my life in your belly. Give me a child."

My heart leaped: Had he discovered the secret infusions that made Amazons sterile? Was that why he had looked at me strangely and grown so angry?

"I want you to give birth to a child in whom our two bloods will be mixed, our minds united, our bodies fused."

His words hammered into my head: Alexander knew nothing of the Great Queen's curse, or of the terrible death that snatches women in childbirth. He did not know that Alestria could lose this war.

"Are you afraid of the pain?" His voice continued to haunt me. "Are you afraid of dying?"

I shuddered: How could he read my thoughts?

"I will be beside you. I will draw the child from your belly. I will bind your wounds and tend you. And then, when we have won that sublime battle, all three of us will sleep together."

I did not know how or where to hide myself, how to disguise my secrets. Alexander was inside me, inside my head, giving me orders:

"Be brave. Without armor or weapons you can still be a warrior. By giving me a child you can conquer death, sweep aside conspirators, and destroy every enemy army. You alone in the whole world can grant me this victory. Don't be afraid! This world is yours. Beauty is you!"

. . .

NEWS OF REVOLTS reached us from the front. We heard of attempts to assassinate the king and of how the conspirators were executed. According to the rumors, Bagoas tirelessly tracked down traitors and potential murderers. People were saying the king no longer consulted his friends but simply forced his army to keep advancing.

The king returned. Alexander, indefatigable, galloped toward his queen, and his queen ran out to meet him. Alestria could smile once more. She shut herself away in her tent with him, refusing to see anyone. She would not eat or drink because eating and drinking were a waste of time: she wanted to stay by his side, to grow drunk on the nearness of him.

But was Alexander truly in love with the queen?

He came back to inspect his rearguard forces. He spent the morning reading missives from all the Alexandrias, and dictating replies. Once his messengers had galloped off, he called in the commanders responsible for supplies. Huddled over maps of the Indies spread on a table in his tent, he discussed military advances with Ptolemy. During the afternoon he did the rounds of the men's quarters, checking their armor and trying out lances and arrows. He stopped by the stables and made inquiries about the breeding program. He brought unfamiliar fabric back to the weavers and explained to them how to make more robust clothes. He asked questions of the farmers and dawdled around his scientists, asking them to read some of their writings to him. He brought them gifts of new species of plants, insects, and animals and new kinds of stone, and together they went into raptures about the diversity of nature. He visited the wounded and lavished them with kind words—so many flattering lies, just like the words he spoke to my queen to ensure that she would endure the waiting patiently. But, comforted by his attentions, these men would get back up and set off for the front again with him to die there.

What he really came back for was to give my queen a child. Alexander furiously fertilized her belly in the hopes of spawning a multitude of descendants. He wanted three boys and three girls, and for those three boys and three girls to bring forth sixty princes to govern his empire. What he wanted, as Darius had before him, was to reign over the world of men forever.

Alexander knew I did not like him. He paid me compliments and gave me gifts. He took it into his head to find me a husband and asked me to choose from among his commanders. I was distracted with rage and humiliation, I, Ania, the queen's intransigent serving woman. I did not like him; I did not even admire him. I loathed him for caging the Amazons who were so wild and free.

I took my revenge on him in secret, keeping quiet the sense of pride it afforded me. When the king left the queen's bed to talk to his soldiers I brought Alestria a double portion of the infusion that made her sterile. The queen of the Amazons would bear no child for the king of warriors. Our bodies were not vehicles for masculine domination—our eternity lay in teaching future generations. Our blood had no ambitions to invade the blood of other peoples—our strength converted them.

Alexander came back. He rested in Alestria's belly, robbing her strength, and then left again. My queen grew thinner: rumors about the obstacles her husband faced had built a nest in her head and laid a clutch of concerns there. She obstinately hid her fears, never complaining about her life of imprisonment. The suffering that burned her and the physical effort she put into silently fighting that fire still managed to make her look radiant. I had never seen my queen more focused or more serene looking. That beauty, sculpted by a combination of pain and dignity, was incomprehensible to Alexander's courtiers. People whispered that she had a lover; they said a young warrior from Thessaly, recently arrived in camp with Greek reinforcements, had seduced the queen with his fresh face and young body not yet damaged in war. They said this Thessalian nobleman was transfixed by the queen; he wanted to steal her from Alexander and run away with her.

As soon as Alexander caught wind of the rumor, he abandoned his army and came galloping back. Almost before he was inside the encampment, the jealous tyrant asked to meet the queen's "lover." His men searched for a long time and reported back that the young man, terrified of Alexander's anger, had already fled with his soldiers. Furious and consumed with jealousy, Alexander dragged Alestria to his tent and asked her to account for herself.

His flashing eyes, roaring voice, and threatening gestures did nothing to impress Alestria, who had decapitated the most brutal of warriors in her time. She listened to his complaints and accusations without replying, which made Alexander angrier still. With tears in his eyes, he pointed at the gifts he had sent her and cried:

"Alestria, I love you! All of these are proof of that. Wherever Alexander's army goes, the most wonderful gems, the most beautiful animals, the most fragrant flowers, and the most dazzling jewels are all for you, the queen of my heart. On the eve of battle, I shut myself in my tent to sort through your gifts, arrange them, choose them, and wrap them myself! In this warrior's life you are an oasis of peace. I only have to think of you for the tumult of battle to stop haunting me and for happiness and peace to return.

"Alestria, I put my thoughts, my dreams, your smiles, and your happiness into each of these things. Here are a pair of crickets I asked to sing for you. At night their song reaches into your dreams, spreading the words of love I taught them. Here is a feather for you to write your poems and send them to me. I want to go to sleep with your voice telling me that, in spite of the distance, you will always love me. Here is a star of crystal that promises us eternal life. Here is a heart-shaped ruby, it is my own heart, which needs to beat close to yours. However ridiculous they may seem to you, these gifts are me! I am all over this tent, and even when I am away I watch over your well-being. You are not alone, Alestria. When you wear these jewels, when you wrap yourself in these tunics, it is me kissing you and holding you in my arms.

"When I die someday, when my god decides to take me from my queen, you will realize that all these things contain a little part of me. And you will have a treasure from me: my eyes, my mouth, my hair, my tears. You will see that I am still there living beside you, all around you, protecting you, loving you even more than in life. For when I am dead, I shall no longer be a warrior. Freed from my earthly duties, I shall devote my days and nights to loving you, to breathing your presence and you breathing mine, to sleeping inside you, waking beside you, living in your eyes, your mouth, your body, and your soul."

In spite of my hatred of Alexander, I, Ania, was moved by his words. Standing by the door to the royal tent, listening in secret, I shed a few tears.

But Alestria, impassive, remained silent.

Alexander fell at her feet, bathing his wife's tunic with his bitter tears.

"You no longer love me, then! You want to leave me for this young man who has not fought! Alestria, forgive me for being away. Don't abandon me!"

My queen's body made a small movement. She took Alexander's face in her hands and stared him right in the eye.

"I want to go into battle! I want to make war by your side. I do not want to be Queen of Asia. I want to defend you and to die for you!"

Alestria's words made me quiver with joy: my queen no longer wanted to live confined to the city. She had deliberately made Alexander jealous of an anonymous soldier—it was her strategy to force her husband to take her into battle.

The king leaped to his feet.

"Never," he cried, "never!"

Alestria pushed him away violently.

"Why not me?" she cried, even more loudly than him. "Why not Alestria, who can fight better than your men?"

"Because you are my queen. A queen is the heart of the empire; she should bear the king's heir," bellowed Alexander. "A queen is someone people venerate. Like a goddess, people whisper her name but do not know her face. You should be an Eastern Athena, inspiring strength, courage, and the union of our peoples."

"I am not some divinity!" Alestria shouted again, trying to be heard by a husband who was deaf to her desires. "I am a warrior who rides faster than any man. Take me with you, Alexander! Disguise me as a man. Ania will agree to take my place and wear my veil. No one will know it is not me. I am leaving with you; I want to stay with you day and night. I want to protect you from arrows drawn to the front, to the left, and to the right. I want to fight with you. Together we can force back the shadows and reach the sun."

My heart leaped: I, Ania, would not wear her royal veil either. I was a warrior, and I had my pride as an Amazon. I would not bury myself alive in this city that supported hordes of eunuchs and women with no muscles, bland dishonest creatures constantly discussing petty intrigues. I too had aspirations to blood, purity, and a glorious death. I would follow Alestria and fight the ape-men, snakes, and crocodiles. I would never be a veiled queen!

But Alexander understood nothing about women. Alexander was so full of his masculine power that he wanted no woman by his side. He did not want his queen to triumph where he had been defeated. He did not want to give Alestria an opportunity to conquer the world with him, for him. He did not love my queen. He looked down on women and thought of us as domestic animals. He threw himself at Alestria and took her in his arms, telling her to stop making these childish requests. He called her his little girl and said he would come back to her more often. He tried to undress her, smiling and telling her that if she loved him she should not die for him but give him a child.

I, Ania, was incensed. Was this love: hiding away a woman as capable of fighting monsters as himself? Was this love: making an Amazon die of boredom and wealth and powerless power? Was this Alexander's love: putting a bird of the glacier in a cage and leaving it there to wither and fade?

Alestria, always so calm and well behaved, was suddenly furious. Interpreting her fury as hysteria, Alexander initially spoke like a patient, indulgent father. But, rather than consoling her, his words only humiliated her further. An Amazon's anger is a fearful thing: she screamed and wept and threw his gifts on the ground. She wanted to go back to the steppes. Having no more clever lies up his sleeve, Alexander too became angry. He blocked the queen's way and roared at her. She took him by the wrists and elbowed him in the stomach, launching him to the ground. He clutched hold of her ankle, tripping her up, then threw himself at her, shouting angrily. She grabbed his throat, but he knocked her out with a powerful clout from his head.

I, Ania, thought with delight that they no longer loved each other and would now part. But their anger was already eroding, the storm was passing, and after the turmoil came the cool, silent night. Alexander took Alestria in his arms and whispered poems of love in her ear.

I wandered through the forest, my heart laden with sorrow as the undergrowth was weighed down by rain. Up in the sky the moon was in its zenith, and the stars had disappeared in its bright light. My queen was like that pure detached moon, forgiving, still shining, still radiant for Alexander, offering him the last of her light.

I kicked out at a tree, and a shower of dew fell from it. Thousands of moons slithered from its leaves and fell, flattened, on the ground.

· · ·

MY BELOVED BLEW on my forehead. I stroked his cheek where it was scratched. He looked at me so searchingly.

"Alestria, you who want to fight," he said with a smile, "do you know about war? You know about wielding weapons, about the smell of blood and the squeals of injured horses, but you do not know war. I don't want you to know it. I don't want you to know the madness of men. You who are pure and transparent as tourmaline sown on the ground by the dawn, I have brought you on my journey, but you must not come into my world. You must not know the world I come from."

I said nothing, listening to him.

"War is hundreds, thousands, of men and horses lined up in icy silence. When the horns sound, they throw themselves at each other. Feathers, arrows, lances, shields, everything becomes confused. Arms fly off, thighs are cut open, feet severed. Heads roll and bellies spew out blood. Men in combat are more ferocious than starving animals devouring each other. Striking blows with lances, axes, hammers, and sabers, they mutilate their enemies and send them to their deaths. While some fall, others march over their bodies and fight on. Then silence, the ground strewn with corpses while fresh blood showers over dried blood. Dying horses tremble till their teeth chatter. Survivors wander among the dead, stealing anything of value. Scavengers are drawn from far and wide to enjoy this feast that will ensure their survival. Flies swarm down from the sky, settling on every excrescence of life: white spilling from open heads; green and yellow tumbling from abdomens; red seeping from chests. They cluster on motionless hands still holding weapons, they cloak rigid feet, feet with broken toenails because they have done too much marching. They lick greedily at a hairy ankle, a thigh speared by an arrow, a torso without a head, and wide-eyed heads without torsos.

"Then comes the pain of seeing all those ashen faces. Then comes the dizzying agony of driving your sword into a friend's heart to spare him a slow death. Then comes the regret of ever having been Alexander, just one man alive among the dead . . ."

It was dark, and I did not move, barely even breathing. Alexander's words tormented me, and my limbs turned to ice in the long silence that followed them.

"War is man's madness!" he went on, his voice mournful. "And I, Alexander, am the flame of that madness. I am the one writing this tragedy that men will still sing about in a thousand years' time. I am a madman suffering this chronic illness and elected by other men like myself. War is an appointment kept by those who thirst for atrocities, an opportunity for them to indulge their longings. . . . When I was twenty I held feasting that went on for days after every battle. I drank to forget death and its fetid smell. I drowned myself in pleasure to rediscover life. At thirty, instead of intoxicating me, these banquets make me sadder still. I would rather shut myself away in my tent alone, far from drunken revelers . . ."

Without a word, I took my husband to our bed. He undressed and huddled in my arms while I gently stroked his back, scored with so many scars it felt like a tortoise's shell.

"I don't want you to know war," he said hoarsely. "You are the best of me. When I am with you I forget the horror of it, I think only of you. War no longer exists, and I am back to the Alexander I once was, the little boy full of dreams."

I kissed his hair, his forehead, his eyes.

"You must not know the dead. They take the shape of flames, dancing before you and laughing at you. You must close your eyes on the madness of this lowly world. Men make war as women make life. I shall take you to the sun itself without your sullying your hands or feet. And some days I want to be alone, hiding in my tent. No one must see me on those dark days when I am afraid and cold. I shiver and wait for the despair to pass, for hope to bloom again, for courage to return. Alestria, I beg you, let me leave as a conqueror and return as a victor. Let me play the role of a warrior who knows no cowardice or suffering. Let me play the role of a king venerated by every people on earth, a king who lends his fine face and well-proportioned body to sculptors from every land to represent the gods. Courage, honor, greatness, and glory are just empty words. Wars are dirty, conquests merely illusion. Those who back away and flee are just as worthy as those who keep on advancing and embrace death. Despair and hope, fear and temerity, reason and madness, are all twins. Only our love is unique."

My husband's last sentence swept aside all the horrors he had told me about himself. Although still reeling from what he had admitted, I could feel the warmth with which Talaxia and Tankiasis had healed my body, battered by the cold and by wounds. I, Alestria, the woman whom my husband had met away from time itself and away from war, I loved him because he was my destiny.

I accepted his madness, his murders, his greatness, and his woes—I accepted them with my eyes open.

"Stop suffering," I told him. "Everything you have just told me will be thrown into the lake that rests deep within my heart. I shall pray for the dead who have finished this life. For them to be born again as birds, free as birds, in the next."

My words soothed Alexander. He pressed his cheek against my breast.

"Sleep, my love. Sleep, my warrior. We are two pilgrims on the road to the glacier. You met me, and I found you. With you in front and me behind, we shall join forces and we will reach the summit."

CHAPTER 10

Alestria had lost her bloom. Her cheeks were no longer rounded, and her eyes had a strange gleam to them. Against her pale face her pupils had become dark stars lit by black flames. I never suspected her condition—for Alexander destroyed everything he touched—until the day I heard two women whispering behind a sheet hanging on a line:

"The queen is with child!"

Alestria with child! I burst into her tent. She was sitting before her mirror, pinning up her hair.

"Is it true that you are with child?"

In the mirror her eyes avoided mine.

"Are you with child?"

She lowered her head and said nothing. I left her tent, smacking the door closed behind me.

Alestria had gone mad; there was no other explanation. Bewitched by Alexander's words, she had decided to renounce our ancestors and put her life in danger for him.

"The queen is with child!" The rumor did the rounds of the city, spreading along trade routes and propagated all over the Indies. I did not believe it: Alexander had invented this to encourage his army to advance, Alestria had imagined it to satisfy a husband increasingly impatient for an heir. It was all just a conspiracy conjured by men who, thanks to this good news, hoped to win back the trust of their soldiers and incite them to fight.

The king arrived, radiantly happy. I greeted his happiness with a heavy heart and an icy expression. Unaware of my anger, the king congratulated me, saying I was to become an aunt. How could Alestria's frail body carry a child? How could that slender silhouette, those narrow hips, deliver a life? How could anyone cheat the curse of our ancestors? I did not understand my queen's smile, or the king's joy. She was going to die: they should have been weeping, but they were laughing!

Alexander ordered three days and three nights of banqueting all over the empire. In our encampment a huge gathering of generals, commanders, soldiers, workmen, seamstresses, and sandal makers swarmed around the fires to drink to the thousand-year reign of the future prince. Alexander was drunk, beating a drum while his monkey—an even more ridiculous creature than the eunuch Bagoas—plucked the strings of a lute. Alestria kept having to withdraw to be sick. I watched the whole devastating spectacle without a word. My queen had betrayed me, but I said nothing to reproach her; I sulked in silence. I continued to serve this woman who had led us into betrayal and captivity, because she was my queen and my sister. To each their own war. To each their own brand of madness. While Alexander fought beyond the frontiers of the known world, Alestria overstepped forbidden boundaries and advanced toward an unknown fate.

She had violent headaches, and still she grew thinner. Unlike some women who grow more beautiful in pregnancy, Alestria grew plain. Brown marks appeared at her temples, her cheeks became gaunt, and her forehead looked disproportionately tall and ponderous. But her husband had regained all his lust for life. Alestria was dying, and Alexander was thriving. He talked loudly, jubilantly, took the queen in his arms, patted her stomach, and boasted about how beautiful she was.

"Look how beautiful my Alestria is!" he exulted, calling me as a witness. Then, not waiting for any remark from me, he added: "Ania, you shall watch over my child! I spent thirty years looking for a queen," he confessed with tears in his eyes. "I rode all the way to Asia to meet her. I survived injury, poisons, the cold, sunstroke, evil spells, and exhaustion to reach the happiness I have today. My god has blessed me, how lucky I am!"

I said nothing. All I could read on my queen's blotchy face were suffering and death. I slipped out of the encampment to stray through the forests. Despite the soldiers' warnings I felt no fear: no tigers or boa constrictors, no ape-men or speaking parrots, could frighten me. Armed with my two daggers forged by the People of the Volcano, I walked on and sat down at the foot of a tree to shed a few tears. Why had my life changed overnight? Why had the vastness of the steppes become the torments of the jungle? Why had the simplicity of the earth and sky become the labyrinth of this forest teeming with smells and colors and sounds? I no longer knew where to find good and where to find evil. I could no longer distinguish between beauty and sadness. Had I lost my mind? Was I, too, haunted by spirits? Where were they taking me? Toward the light or toward the shades?

I wept again and again until all the despair was emptied out of me and hope filled me once again. Then I wiped away my tears and went back to the tented city, to Alexander and Alestria. Although lost in my own distress, I knew that the God of Ice had not abandoned me. He was making me tackle a slope where the north wind blew hard and night seemed to go on forever.

In the past Alestria had led the troop of Amazons, and I, Ania, had galloped behind her without a care in the world.

Now my god had separated me from my queen.

With no guide, with no friend, alone, I had to climb the glacier.

. . .

IN THE LAND of the Indies night was dark and the moon icy. The river Hydaspe whispered in the distance while a Persian soldier played the flute nearby.

I had seized the Birdless Rock that resisted Hercules in ancient times. This conquest was a more dazzling exploit than the twelve labors accomplished by the son of Zeus. From now on no hero and no mortal could act as an example for Alexander.

I was slipping into the infinity of the universe, oppressed and yet comforted by solitude. I could still hear Philip's howls and Olympias's weeping. I could still hear my own impassioned speeches and the bustle of soldiers marching toward Persia. But they were now merely the feeble echo of previous lives. Countless battles had raised me to the world of the night and sparkling lights. Far from earthly fates, up in the star-filled sky, I had no friends anymore, no troops. I heard neither their calls nor their cries. I was accompanied by silence, sometimes threatening, sometimes soothing. Death had never felt so close, but I was less hostile to its company. It was once a constant threat, but now I saw it as the accomplishment of my person, as release for my army. I trusted the gods who had granted me the time to wage war, and I waited for the final day when death would make me immortal.

Alestria's belly was growing. I had an heir! The thought of it worried me and filled me with joy. Would I be a good father? Would I have my mother's patience and Aristotle's wisdom? Would I be able to make of him a courageous and well-reasoned prince? How could I bequeath him this vast empire I myself had never succeeded in governing?

I had always desired strong young men; they were like so many rocks strewn along my way, tackled with tact and determination. Born in different lands and brought up in different cultures, some understood the calendar of the stars, others counted using sticks or had their own strange way of saddling horses. Each of them harbored a hidden treasure, unwritten poetry, an understanding of the birth of the world. Once we were naked, our differences melted away. Male flesh is a wild land in which no civilization and no religion has ever taken seed. Two men together is a meeting with oneself; it is confrontation and physical gratification in step with each other.

Alestria was not my reflection. I understood nothing of her body, even less of this growing belly. I did not seek gratification in her: I united myself with her strength, which perpetuated life.

I found Alestria disconcerting; her metamorphosis amazed me, frightened me, and fascinated me. I kept taking her in my arms, breathing in the smell of her and touching her swelling breasts. Her hair was becoming dry, her cheeks blotchy, her lips cracked. All these flaws, like the impurities of the moon, served only to make her shine more brightly.

I begged her to undress, and lay next to her, fingering this body in which another body was germinating. I pressed my ear to her stomach and listened to the rustling of a new world. I looked between her legs and wondered how my son would reach me through that tiny channel. I was gripped by a nameless fear, nauseous and vertiginous. I felt even more vulnerable and disarmed than my pregnant queen. I was afraid she might trip, afraid of conspiracies; I could not leave her side. I took her everywhere with me and settled her where my eyes could always alight on her. Her presence reassured me. She and our child, they were all that was left of my journey toward the future.

Inside a man's body I surrendered to a war of pleasure. The struggle was a game of balance, a dance of well-mastered movements. In Alestria's belly I was absorbed, I became clumsy. I carried her heavy body on my back; she held me to her breasts swollen with milk. We flew together through the night. We flew together toward the dawn.

. . .

ALESTRIA HAD STOPPED talking of going to the front. Alexander had succeeded in holding his queen back by giving her a child. She had stopped waiting for the king outside the city gates but stayed calmly in her tent talking to her belly. She spent her time sewing children's clothes, but she was not gifted with a needle. She sewed so badly that her servants secretly unpicked her work and pieced it together again. Unaware of her ineptitude, my queen took pleasure in her sewing.

Having always been distant with the warriors' wives, she now started spending time with them and asking them about child-birth. Women were eager to give her advice, to offer her particular food and drink, and to shower her with flattery, which made her smile dreamily.

The king interrupted his campaigns to watch over her. I saw the loathsome Bagoas prowling around our city once more. He had grown even fatter, his double chin gleaming amid the soldiers' thin, honed faces. Alexander had brought back an army sickened and demoralized by wind, rain, and arrows.

The city was abuzz with drumming, singing, and banqueting once more. The king and his men drank to the birth of his heir. Alestria wore a veil to receive their compliments, and I stood behind her, knowing she was tired and suffering.

But Alestria was proud, and she wanted to please the man she loved. She stood close to him like a faithful sentry. Back in her tent, she fell asleep exhausted, but the king, who was always over-flowing with ideas and energy, would not let her rest. He woke her so soon, asking her to go with him to inspect his army or to watch them in training: he was devising a new plan of attack.

Worn down by such demands, she fainted. She was brought back to our quarters, and I, Ania, fussed over her to bring her round. She woke slowly, looking lost, as if she had been on a long journey. The king sent messengers to inquire how she was, and these boorish soldiers—who had been given instructions to see her with their own eyes—argued with me at the door of her tent. Alestria rose to her feet, changed her clothes, and asked to be taken to her husband. Alexander was a pitcher full of cool fresh water, and she wanted to drink it down to the last drop.

Alestria's belly swelled while her body grew thinner. It was such a small belly! Compared to the great mountains borne by other pregnant women, hers was a tiny hill. Unaware of its meager volume, the king and queen went into ecstasies every time they looked at it.

They spent hours admiring that belly. Alexander stroked it and pressed his cheek up against it, speaking to her navel. Alestria lay smiling, and she too stroked it, answering for her belly. The king and queen conversed through that belly, both laughing and crying, both forgetting that it was abnormally small, both believing that from this minute hill a great man would be born.

They argued over his name. They argued over each item of clothing he would wear. They argued over the choice of tutor: Alexander wanted to summon Aristotle, while Alestria did not want it to be a man.

Alexander sought out midwives, not trusting any of the women in his entourage. The queen's belly had become the focus of all intrigues and plots. Everyone knew that the birth of an heir would annihilate the generals' hopes of acceding to the throne in the event of Alexander's death. In the end he conceived the extraordinary idea of entrusting this task to Bagoas. I, Ania, screamed with indignation.

Bagoas, that glistening worm! Bagoas, who slept with men to sound out how loyal they were to the king? Bagoas the informer, the spy, the torturer who was neither man nor woman? He would not touch my queen's little toe! It would be I, Ania, I the Amazon, who drew this child from that belly, despite the curse of our ancestors.

. . .

I CANNOT TELL you where I come from, my child. In the early days of my life, I crawled among wild horses, drinking a mare's milk when I was hungry and thirsty. I pulled at her mane and heaved myself onto her back, then clung to her neck as she galloped. My first mother smelled of sunlight, grass, and dung. She licked me from head to foot and showed her yellow teeth when she laughed. Under the starry sky of the steppes she slept on her feet with me between her legs. She taught me that language is a music and that whoever opens their heart to the music understands the language of grasshoppers, butterflies, birds, wolves, and trees.

One day nomads appeared on the horizon and chased us for days on end. One after another the horses were captured with a long rope, and I was taken to the chief's wife. My second mother taught me to dress myself and walk with shoes. She burrowed me under a blanket with her children, and I escaped at night to sleep outside the tent under the stars. One evening I was woken by the thunder of hooves: horsemen brandishing sabers descended on our tents, killing the whole tribe in their sleep and stealing their horses and cattle. Hiding in a bush with my hands over my ears, I saw and heard nothing. I lived among the corpses until the day another tribe passed and put me up on a horse's back, but I never stayed with my adoptive families after that, leaving them after one season. I was too afraid of seeing them massacred by the horsemen galloping out of the huge opening between the earth and the sky.

One day I heard the legend of the Amazons who had no fear of men, and I wanted to be like them. I walked alone toward the north of the steppes. Three seasons later an Amazon discovered me and took me to their queen. She undressed me, pointed at the scar on my breast, and wept tears of joy. I do not remember where that scar came from. It looks like an iron branding or an animal bite. It is the secret inscribed by the God of Ice.

I did not see my mother Talaxia very often. It was a time of great upheaval: the tribes on the steppes fought constantly with each other. After several seasons of drought, good pastureland was rare, and horses and cattle were starving. Men turned to pillaging.

The queen disappeared frequently, and I was raised by Tankiasis, her serving woman, whom I called my aunt. It was she who fed me with goat's and cow's milk. Sometimes we had to break camp and gallop for days on end, pursued by our attackers. She tied me against her chest, and I rested my head between her breasts. Sometimes we were the ones who launched an attack, and then she would tie me to her back. I could feel her muscles tensing and relaxing. I clung to her heat and sweat, listening to the war cries reverberating through her body, and dozing to the clash of weapons and the whinnying of horses.

My aunt smelled of goat's milk and chrysanthemums. In summer I liked to lick the salt from her skin while she fanned me with large leaves and sung me tunes of the steppes. When my mother returned, her mare's hooves made the ground shake, and the pungent smell of unknown lands preceded her. She leaned over me and pinched my cheeks. She gave orders in her powerful voice, and all the girls started packing up: we had to leave. Every time my mother appeared, it was the sign for another departure. I was afraid of her; I did not want to leave. I wanted to stay between my aunt's breasts, at peace, forever.

My mother was strong and brutal, my aunt tender and gentle. Talaxia rode horses and fought with men. Tankiasis managed the girls and defended me. She brought me up to be intrepid and spontaneous as the queen, and tender and thoughtful as her serving woman. I am the fruit of two women who were sisters and lovers. I am the fruit of their love, which ended only when, one after the other, they left this lowly world.

One day I saw my mother return with one breast pierced by an arrow embellished with green feathers. My aunt called for a large pyre to be built and for Talaxia's body to be laid on top of it. With her hair awry and her body covered in sweat, she prostrated herself before that fire for several days.

Talaxia and Tankiasis had met when they were still young. My aunt had been married to a tribal chief, one of many wives living on colorful soft carpets in a vast tent. She had left her husband and her child, betrayed her family, abandoned her servants, torn her beautiful clothes, and handed out her jewels. She left in the middle of a dark night, on the back of a mare belonging to a woman known as the queen of Siberia. Talaxia and Tankiasis loved each other and never left each other. But my mother was not faithful; she made other seductions and had countless lovers, both men and women. She brought home other young women frantic with desire and admiration for her. Tankiasis—who had given up her original name, her mother, her sisters, and her child—accepted all these hardships because of that extraordinary emotion called love.

Tankiasis crouched before the pyre while the flames danced in her eyes. Her queen was no more: Talaxia, the indefatigable warrior, conqueror of men and women, would never seduce again. She had abandoned everything she had conquered, abandoned all her prey and her harvests, in order to travel up to the skies along that pillar of black smoke.

My aunt stayed by the pyre until the last spark faltered and went out. She took the decision to stay for my sake, to finish her instruction, to teach me the silent prayers that respond to the call of the glacier. Then one morning she left without a trace. Tankiasis went to join Talaxia among the stars, leaving me with an enigma: What is love? Is it a song with no odor or color or melody, but which bewitches the living and the dead?

My child, you carry in your veins all the patience of Tankiasis, who stitched every one of my garments, and the strength of Talaxia, who trained me on horseback. Are their souls rejoicing up there in the wind, the rain, and the zigzag of lightning? The fruit of their love has found fulfillment and now carries the fruit of a love with the king of warriors. You, my child, you in turn will bear fruit, and so the tribe of lovers will be perpetuated.

Ania is afraid of love and suffering, but she will help me bring you into the world. She will raise you, and you will call her your aunt. She will teach you the secrets of the Amazons, and you will teach her to love the volcano, which is just as tall and ardent as the glacier.

My child, you will be strong, courageous, and sensual as your father. You will be calm, reflective, and inspired as your mother.

You will take command of the army when your parents grow old. You will continue to open up roads in a world where there are no roads. You will wear the laurels of warrior men and know the language of warrior women. You will be a tiger and a bird, a king and a queen.

I am waiting for you, my child! Your father is impatient for you to be here! I can feel you moving, you kick so hard it hurts, you strike me with your fists, butt me with your head . . . you make my own head spin.

My child, you leap and bite and tear my flesh!

You cannot wait to be born, you cannot wait to sit in your father's arms, you cannot wait to become a soldier and meet your queen!

My child, I want all the treasures of this world for you, I want a life of battles for you, I want every bird and every horse for you.

When strength withdraws from our bodies, when Alexander and Alestria leave, hand in hand, to join glorious souls among the stars, you will be our flame, our word, our eyes.

My child, Alexandrias, sleep now. Sleep and have beautiful dreams, sleep and have a wondrous awakening!

Sleep, my child, you shall be king of the steppes, forests, and plains, queen of deserts, rivers, and oceans.

Sleep, my child, sleep peacefully. I pray that the God of Ice will send you a beautiful wife.

· · ·

IN THE HEART of the night the female's arms and legs thrash like tentacles. Her vagina opens like a carnivorous plant and slowly spits out a head, a hand, a foot. A life emerges. Blood streams. And in the middle of it the whitish cord. I seize it. I look for the knife to cut it, but it slips from my fingers. I reach for it. The child is already coiling in the gelatinous cord and strangling itself.

I wake with tears in my eyes. I, Ania, loathed the work of a midwife! I loathed myself for witnessing several births so that I would be ready for the queen! The Amazons were right to refuse this thankless task. Why was Alestria insisting on producing an heir when there were so many women crawling round Alexander who could have carried one instead of her? Why was she waging this pointless battle when other more experienced women could have won the fight for her?

The door to my tent was torn open, and one of the girls of Siberia ran in.

"The queen's in labor!" she cried.

I leaped up and ran barefoot to the queen's tent. Alestria was lying on the carpet, racked by violent convulsions. She had torn her tunic and was thrashing and moaning, trying to get to her feet and falling back down onto her back.

I asked for a fire to be lit and for water to be boiled. Two strong girls took Alestria's arms, and two more pinned down her legs. The queen bit into a cushion and stifled her cries, but her sweat-soaked body and distraught expression communicated her pain to me. I examined her inside: there was a trickle of blood, but the channel was not yet open.

It was daybreak. The blood had stopped flowing, but the suffering did not abate. She was trembling, and her eyes were wide and full of tears. The entire city had been drawn to the spectacle: women gathered outside the tent and, behind them, crowds of soldiers. Their commanders came to speak to me, but I waved them away impatiently. No one was authorized to come into the queen's tent. A few days earlier Alexander had left the city in great haste, and no one knew where he was or when he would return. Without the king there, I was suspicious of every man's motives. I, Ania, armed the girls of our tribe and positioned them round the tent to protect Alestria.

My queen's stifled cries cut me to the core. She fainted after each convulsion. The army's best midwife came to help me. She palpated Alestria's belly for a long time and then told me we would have to kill the queen to save the child, for out of the mother and the heir, there would be only one survivor.

If only one of them was to live, it would be my queen. I had the madwoman thrown out of the tent.

The sun sank in the sky. Now exhausted, the monster Alestria bore granted her a moment's respite. I washed the queen's body and covered her in a clean tunic. In the middle of the night the convulsions returned and the blood began to flow again. Having pulled the cushion to pieces, Alestria asked for a sheet to muffle her cries. It was not long before she lost her voice and, her mouth wide with pain, made a mewling sound. I fell to the ground beside her and prayed. Where are you, God of Ice? Save Alestria! Save my queen! Take my life instead of hers!

Day took over from the night. My queen could no longer cry, she lay there panting.

Ptolemy introduced a sorcerer renowned for his powerful magic, which had saved kings and princes of the Indies. With his wrinkled face, his protruding yellowish eyes and earlobes distended by earrings laden with diamonds, he looked like an old woman. He wore a pleated skirt around his hips, and his scrawny arms were covered in gold bangles set with rubies. He examined Alestria and told me he could save the mother.

"Yes, my queen must be saved!" I told him. "Alexander will give you ten chariots filled with bracelets and earrings if you drive death from this tent."

The sorcerer boiled herbs, roots, and dried fruit in water. He sang as he stirred the concoction with a black spoon, and made signs with his free hand. Even the bitter smell of his infusion seemed to soothe the laboring mother. I ordered the sorcerer to taste his medicine, which could have contained poison, then blew over the bowl until the liquid had cooled before bringing it to Alestria's lips.

She refused to open her mouth.

I shook her and begged her, wasting my breath trying to persuade her. Reluctantly, I cited Alexander's love for her and the possibility of another child. But Alestria, the intrepid warrior, did not back away from death. She kept her teeth clenched, would not admit defeat. Haunted by the legend of the Great Queen, who died in childbirth, I wept streams of tears.

Suddenly Alestria moved and opened her eyes. I ran over to lift her up and offer her the infusion. She looked at me tenderly, smiling and shaking her head.

Gripped by anger, I threw caution to the wind and cried:

"Let him go! He's a monster! He wants to kill the mother and control the father. He wants to annihilate Alexander and Alestria in order to be the one king of every land! Condemn him. Turn your back on him. Look at the light and turn toward our god."

"I am already in the light!" she murmured.

In her weak, halting voice she explained that Talaxia, Tankiasis, and all the dead warrior women had come down from the skies. They had gathered in that tent and were waiting for the arrival of the great king.

She was delirious. She had been taken over by evil spirits who wanted to bear her away. Night drove out the day. I sat beside my queen with two daggers in my lap, cursing Alexander for abandoning her. I was powerless, listening to the rustle of the wind and night birds chattering and sniggering. Alestria's body was racked with shaking and already looked as fragile as a pile of dead leaves.

I greeted the dawn when it returned at last. My eyes scanned the inside of that tent and came to rest on the trunk full of Alexander's gifts. I stood up stiffly and took those jewels and trinkets that had brought my queen so much joy and sadness, and laid them out around her inert body. I put my hand on her belly: the child had stopped moving. The monster had not found its path to life. Alestria, the invincible warrior, had lost this battle that so many other women would have won.

Now I, Ania, who had not slept for three days, saw an army of lost souls. They had come for Alestria. Oh, that they would take me with my queen!

Alestria's hands were cold as ice. She was still breathing, but her soul had left her body. She was there among those wild spirits who loved victory and light, laughing, dancing, and occasionally peering at me out of curiosity.

Alestria, it is I, Ania, your sister, your servant, your scribe!

Alestria, have you forgotten those flat stones on which we started writing our story?

Alestria, have you forgotten the smell of lily of the valley, the song of the white birds, the gold and red clouds rising on the horizon?

Alestria, are you weary of Alexander, the man who brought an end to your galloping and who showed you all the pleasure and pain of being a woman?

Alestria, come back! The life of kings is an illusion. We can return to our own land and go back to our novel of the stars.

Come back to your body, Alestria!

• • •

POROS. THE NAME obsessed me. People everywhere praised his intelligence and fine looks. His reputation for eloquence had spread along the banks of the Indus: he alone succeeded in rallying the princes to drive Alexander back out of their lands.

I had left my queen to fight this fearsome rival. I offered pacts to the cities I had conquered, and promised those that surrendered the fertile lands that belonged to Poros. Right in the heart of the web woven for me by my adversary, I was building my own net. Where he had found friendship, I set up an army. In my progress toward the south I knew that Poros was riding out on his white elephant, sometimes ahead of me, sometimes following behind me. Neither he nor I had yet chosen when we would meet. But the battle was already inscribed in the stars.

That night I saw Ania in my dreams. She was staring at me, her eyes full of hate, and hissing: "Alexander, the queen is dead."

I woke. It was not yet light outside. It was raining, and I thought I heard moaning from the queen I had abandoned for the toils of war. "Alexander, come back!" Ania, her faithful servant, called. "The queen is in labor! It's a boy!"

Alexander must not turn his back on war for a woman! He must show his soldiers that he can sacrifice his family for the sake of victory.

Kristna, a young Indian prince, had secretly sent me a message offering me an alliance against Poros on condition that I left him his fields of *hashna*, the grass of happiness. Was this offer a trap or an opportunity? Was it bait put out by Poros or the whim of a prince who wanted to play one warrior king off against another? I drove Alestria and Ania from my mind and concentrated on the lands of the Indies reconstructed in miniature on the table before me. Different-colored stones represented the various kingdoms spread out between the forests and mountains. Blue was for allies, yellow for adversaries, and green for those who had not yet chosen between Alexander and Poros.

I ordered my men to break camp and rode out at the head of my army toward Kristna's enemies. By killing them I could offer this prince a poisoned gift: he would have to ally himself to me, he would no longer have any choice.

Nothing—not Alestria's tears nor the birth of my child— must interrupt my progress. Nothing must slow me down or break my concentration. I shall race headlong toward this duel, this great battle.

I was haunted by Alestria's pale face. The dark foliage looked like her naked body giving birth. A snake the color of fire flew in front of me and bit a guard, killing him instantly. Hephaestion had toothache, and his gum was so swollen he could no longer talk. All these signs were bad omens and made me anxious. Alestria, forgive me, I am riding toward our glory! I am fighting for your beauty, for your radiance, for the future reign of our child! Alestria, do not weep. I shall return when I have won the battle. I shall return to give you Poros's white elephant and a river of diamonds.

The rain stopped, the wind blew, and the river Hydaspe roared. I heard Ania's voice accusing me: Why did you beget a child if you are afraid of being a father? Why have you abandoned your wife like every other Alexandria you conquered? What have you done with your life? You killed your father, rejected your mother, burned every land you passed through! You claim you want the sun but forge your way through the shades.

I galloped along the riverbank, fleeing this voice by urging my horse on, always faster. No, Ania, I am not an ordinary son, husband, or father. I am Alexander the conqueror, I am a phoenix flying above the flames, I am the man who brings about a new world, I am the son of Apollo and the father of all mixed-race children. Ania laughed bitterly and spat out these words: Then Alestria will die. She too will be a part of this charred path you leave behind you. You will stand alone with no wife, no heir, and no army. You will be a star condemned to flee, never knowing any rest. You will burn in a sky that never sees the light, in a frozen darkness where boundaries constantly retreat. You will slip away ever further, ever faster, ever more desperately into those eternal shades!

I pulled on the reins and stopped Bucephalus's frantic galloping. About turn! The king will return to the queen's city! Shouts of joy went up from the army, and soldiers hurried back to the encampment to hot meals, dry beds, and their wives' arms.

I galloped out in front, ahead of these men who no longer wanted to make war.

Alestria, Alexander is coming back to you. Alexander is on his way.

．　．　．

"THE KING IS on his way!" A hundred horsemen stormed into the city, calling for the great gates to be opened. Behind the walls, men and women spilled out of their tents and ran toward the road. Crowds formed on both sides of the road, bubbling with excitement like boiling water. The cries and whinnying drew closer; soon the clinking of weapons could be heard. The king is on his way, the king is galloping right up to the royal tent. The king lifts the door of the tent, the king is in the middle of this tomb where I, Ania, have lain prostrated for three days.

I did not move, just held Alestria's hand.

I heard Alexander's anxious voice:

"The queen? How is the queen?"

I did not look up and left a moment's silence before replying:

"The queen is dead."

Alexander pushed me aside and threw himself at Alestria's inert body. He shook her and screamed her name, his harrowing cries piercing my ears:

"Alestria, wake up! Alestria, come back! Alestria, don't abandon me!"

He stood back up abruptly, glowered at me, and bellowed:

"Get out! Alestria is mine. You won't have her. Leave us! Go back to where you came from!"

He drew his dagger from his belt and started thrashing the air with it as if fighting invisible warriors. The king had lost his mind.

In a flash I saw Alestria's lips quiver. I took her hand, and she moved slightly. The queen is alive! The queen has come back to us! I laughed and wept all at once, and fought with Alexander to kiss her forehead, her lips. The queen half opened her eyes.

Alestria had forgiven Alexander. She had come back for him.

"Abandon the child!" he ordered her. "It is you that I love!"

Alestria heard his soft but authoritative voice and obeyed her beloved king: she gave up the fight. She drank the infusion prepared by the sorcerer and that night was delivered of a boy. Neither she nor Alexander wanted to touch his cold, shriveled body. It was I, Ania, who wrapped the infant in white cloth, left the city, and went deep into the forest.

On and on I walked while the brightly colored eyes of wild animals flitted around me. I was not afraid and felt no pain. I walked until I came to a river. To us, the Amazons, watercourses were the revelation of the God of Ice. I untied the swaddling, spread the white cloth on the grass, and laid the naked body on it. Even though he was a boy, the son of the queen of the Amazons belonged to our god. I backed away: soon wild animals would eat his flesh and lick his bones; his body would return to the earth while his soul rose up to the heavens. This soul, which was more fierce than Alexander and more persevering than Alestria, had just been too eager, in too much of a hurry. Glory and strength and beauty were waiting for that soul, but our god had decided it should climb the glacier naked.

Wait, wait a little longer, my sister soul. Trust in our god; he will give you another life, another destiny.

· · ·

ALEXANDER DID NOT wait until Alestria had completely recovered before breaking camp and riding out at the head of his army. To everyone's amazement, a covered carriage followed behind the military procession: the queen was accompanying the king. Nearby I, Ania, proudly led the twenty-nine girls of Siberia, complete with helmets and weapons.

The army snaked through the forest before spreading out over a plain where spiny yellow bushes blossomed from the ocher and black soil. The undulating silhouette of a mountain range appeared on the horizon, and birds hovered dizzyingly high above, tiny specks and dashes of movement. By the banks of the river, which had shrunk in recent droughts, near-naked men toiled through the mud, forming a long black line right out into the glinting silver waters. A hundred times, a thousand times they plunged their bamboo sieves into the river, shook them, making the sand and pebbles twinkle, then fingered through the contents before throwing them away.

The mountains drew nearer and grew taller. The forest—full of dark greens, oranges, and pinks—opened up to us and revealed Kristna's city, built vertically on a south-facing flank of the mountain. The ramparts wound their way through the trees, surrounding thatched houses on stilts and others made of beaten earth, while the track climbed and zigzagged to the very top, where a fortress rose into the skies, attracting clouds of birds.

In the gateway stood richly attired soldiers playing the flute and burning incense. They stepped aside to let Alexander and his queen pass, showering them with fragrant petals. To demonstrate his peaceful intentions, the King of Asia had stationed his army far from the town, and his only entourage was made up of the queen's thirty serving women, all of them veiled so that no one would suspect the daggers attached to their belts.

Prince Kristna's fortress was itself the size of a town, flaunting its countless palaces built one above the other. A long covered gallery linked their terraced gardens and ornamental ponds. Borne on sedan chairs, Alexander and Alestria made their way through this steeply raked labyrinth where the women wore dazzling, brightly colored cloth wound around them; they had rings in one nostril, a red spot drawn in the middle of their smooth foreheads, and a black line penciled in under their dark eyes. They greeted the visitors by bowing and joining their hands, which were embellished with red paint, then backed away to the clinking of their countless bangles and the tinkle of bells knotted round their ankles, leaving in their wake their perfume of white flowers.

Well-muscled young men came to greet us, some wearing turbans that were less dramatic than the Persians', others with their black curls falling freely. They wore fine cloth about their waists and knotted between their legs, where it floated in the wind. Some had scars, others not. Some wore bangles on their left forearms; others had diamonds embedded in their noses and earrings. As I saw more of these men, I realized that the number of bangles set with rubies and pearls was a mark of each warrior's courage, an honor granted by their prince.

Our procession passed a spiral of palaces and arrived in a banqueting hall. The high-vaulted ceiling, encrusted with gemstones, was held up by columns of finely carved marble depicting fruit trees, waterfalls, and exotic birds. The walls were paneled with precious wood edged with gold, and against this background were bas-relief scenes carved in ivory: heroes on horseback, legendary cities, and fabulous animals. Kristna, the young prince, who wore a well-groomed mustache, came over to Alexander and welcomed him with his hands joined.

The two men sat down, one at each end of a very long table. With his painted eyebrows and lips and the red powder emphasizing his cheeks, our host looked like a statuette completely covered in precious stones. A dozen necklaces coiled round his neck, covering his chest, which was squeezed into a tight tunic of silver cloth with gold threads woven through it. There was an emerald the size of an egg at the front of his turban, which dripped with white and pink pearls. The narrow sleeves of his tunic gleamed, although they could not compete with the truly remarkable piece of jewelry the prince wore on his right forearm: a wide gold cuff engraved with gods and goddesses dancing in a forest where monkeys, peacocks, tigers, and elephants played with rubies, pearls, and emeralds. Around his narrow waist he wore a belt shaped like a lotus flower, every petal stitched with diamonds and hung with miniature figures. He sat with one leg folded beneath him and rested one arm nonchalantly on the other leg. His foot peeped out from beneath his tunic: there was a ring on every toe, and one of these rings had a tiny cage made of gold holding minute precious stones.

He clapped his hands, and beautiful young serving men filed in, distributed quantities of little silver dishes over the table, then withdrew. Male and female dancers accompanied by musicians appeared and twirled between the columns, jingling the bells on their ankles.

At the other end of the table Alexander pretended to eat and drink, but his lips barely touched his goblet, so afraid was he of being poisoned. That day he wore a scarlet tunic decorated down the front with three phoenixes in embossed gold thread; its wings had taken the most skilled Persian embroiderers three months to complete. His jewels conceded nothing in magnificence to those of the Indian prince, for it was important on this occasion to fight his opponent in wealth, not in power. That is why Alexander had put on ten rings, bearing fiery diamonds, rubies, and emeralds. His turban was wound round with gold thread hung with masses of dazzling precious stones from every corner of the world that Alexander the Great had conquered. Each countless sparkle of jewelry—tiger's eye, moonstone, coral, turquoise, agate, amethyst, pearl, onyx, not to mention the beautiful sapphires and still other stones as yet unknown to man—represented the countless territories he owned. On his feet he wore leather sandals embroidered with gold and stitched with myriad tiny pearls.

The Indian prince had seated his wives behind him, and each of them carried a small tray full of delicacies. These twenty young women—all of them beautiful and alluring—were of many different nationalities, and to counter them Alexander had only Alestria, who had also been given a small low table. She wore a white veil that covered her from head to foot, and one could see only her eyes emphasized with blue in the Persian style. On her head she wore a wreath adorned with the most beautiful diamonds in the world, the size of quail's eggs, and the most talented craftsmen had spent ten years cutting their glittering inner facets, smoothing their outer shapes. Alestria wore no other jewelry, but still she was radiant, making all the other women pale in comparison. Prince Kristna immediately recognized these legendary diamonds that no one but the Great Kings of Persia could ever own. He was besotted with jewelry and could not help constantly commenting on their purity.

The dishes had barely been put on the table before they were cleared away and replaced by other delicacies. A hundred or more plates graced the king's table that evening. As the night wore on the dancers wore fewer and fewer clothes: bare-breasted, they spun round the fountains, skipped down the alabaster steps, or strolled among peacocks and parrots. In the huge gardens torches and candles lit a flower bed of exotic blooms, their petals either ruffled or smooth, thick or thin, opaque or transparent. Each of them was shown off at its best by the ingenious lighting, thanks to which even the leaves competed in this pageant of beauty. Hundreds of different types of leaves—long and slender, short and notched, round and thick—stood out against the darkness and quivered as the dancers brushed past them.

Indian warriors brandishing swords erupted onto the steps. I, Ania, and the queen's Amazon guards ran to meet them with our daggers raised. They started dancing, and we danced with them by way of combat. Kristna's eyes shone; he was watching Alexander: the king, unruffled, smiled and clapped in time to the music.

The sun rose, and the banquet came to an end in feigned drunkenness and mutual mistrust. The two kings exchanged a good many polite niceties, bringing their hands together at chest height, touching their foreheads, and patting each other's shoulders with their left hands while keeping their right hands over their hearts. Kristna accompanied Alexander to the gates of the city, where Hephaestion was waiting for him impatiently. To thank him for such a sumptuous reception, Alexander called for two soldiers to offer his host a pair of gold-plated silver caskets.

Inside them were two severed heads: astonishment turned to smiles when the Indian prince recognized them; then he knelt and swore loyalty to Alexander.

What was it that happened between those two men who barely spoke to each other all evening? I was told that the king had killed the Indian prince's sworn enemies before visiting him. Now hated by the Indian tribes, Kristna was forced to follow Alexander.

As soon as we were back at the encampment, Alestria lay down beside Alexander, and the two lovers spent the day asleep.

Alestria was exhausted.

Alexander was relieved.

• • •

THE ARMY SET up camp and broke camp. We were hounded by groups of Indian warriors: arrows fell, elephants trumpeted, and men screamed in their native languages. These skirmishes erupted more rapidly than summer storms and abated just as quickly. Everyone knew that the king was marching toward one murderous battle. He had an appointment with Poros, a fine, strong Indian king. The two men had never met but had loathed each other through intermediary wars. Each of them had sworn he would have his rival's head and, with it, glory and immortality.

Rivers grew wider, becoming major waterways, and in between them paddy fields flashed like mirrors beneath the sky. Forests surrounded us, then opened out, only to swallow us up again in the shadows of their giant trees. The king rode, and the queen went with him. Side by side they marched toward the greatest war that Indian soil had ever seen.

Alexander gathered his troops on the banks of the Hydaspe.

The wide, peaceful river with its muddy waters glinted yellow. Soldiers and horses arrived along the earth track and down the river. Slaves set out from the encampment with picks. The king disappeared for days on end, and every time he returned, another regiment left to take up its position in the forest.

Alexander had set up a table in his tent, and on it he had had a model of the entire region made with its forests, rocks, rivers, and swamps. I, Ania, who slept in front of the tent to ensure the king and queen's safety, saw Alexander's shadow bending over that table. I could see Alestria's silhouette when she woke and joined her husband. Their two shadows met and forged into one. I no longer tried to decipher signs: I did not want to read the future. Alexander had sought out his wife in the kingdom of souls, and Alestria had followed him and come back to earth. According to steppe tradition, they were both already dead. They were both now living outside time.

Along the river crocodiles floated among broken branches, dead leaves, and pink water lilies. Tree trunks transformed into junks came and went, trailing long wakes of tiny eddies. A moon waxed and waned. Hephaestion, so calm by nature, grew nervous. Bagoas, always edgy and talkative, stopped chattering. Cassander thundered up on his horse, took his orders, and set off again. Persian commanders filed past in the same way. At night there were many sounds against the backdrop of rustling leaves: drum rolls, the wail of horns, and the cries of birds flying off in panic. I lay on my carpet with my ear to the ground, and heard heavy footsteps that made the very earth tremble. Poros and his allies were drawing close. Leading his elephants, the ape-men, and the best warriors in the Indies, Poros was marching on Alexander.

I coped badly with the heat and humidity and could not sleep. I got up and, by moonlight, sharpened the two daggers beaten by the People of the Volcano till their blades gleamed.

•   •   •

THE EARTH RUMBLED, the forest shook, huge ancient trees parted like reeds. Monkeys and birds threw themselves into the air with piercing shrieks. Poros used drugs on his white elephants, and now they hurled themselves at Alexander's army. The soldiers fled while Cassander, dressed all in red, galloped at the head of the cavalry. Fired by the movement of troops, the enraged elephants chased the horses, trumpeting and trampling everything in their way. Cassander's division surged on into an almost dry riverbed, and, following them, the elephants sank into the sludge. Suddenly the waters swelled and changed into a torrent, spilling over the monsters and bearing them away. This was Alexander's doing: he had secretly had a dam built upstream and given Cassander orders to lure the elephants into the trap.

Columns of black smoke rose up and carved through the sky. Fires consumed vines and leaves, climbed up tree trunks, and spat out showers of sparks. Alexander had set fire to the forest, turning it into a labyrinth of flames. His troops marched along strips of land protected by trenches they had dug; they breached Poros's surrounding defenses and cut his army to pieces.

The massacre began. I, Ania, had been given orders by my queen to protect Alexander from any arrows that could potentially be aimed at him by his own generals. He was disguised as an ordinary cavalry soldier as he launched himself at the Indians, screaming. I was dressed as a man and followed behind him, brandishing my weapons. In all that furious killing I forgot the steppes, the birds, and my queen—whose husband had forbidden her to take part in battle. Riding on behind Alexander like his shadow, I lost count of how many Indians I brought down. Furious galloping alternated with pauses during which we wiped off blood, bandaged wounds, and ate hunks of bread. The nights were short: after we snatched some sleep the dawn was already there, casting its white light over the trees while the horns and drums sounded again, urging the men to kill each other to the last one standing.

Alexander searched frantically for Poros, but this war of kings was also a battle of look-alikes. In the distance I saw a number of Alexanders wearing his armor and riding various Bucephaluses. They chased after Poroses in their narrow chariots. For two days now the real King of Asia had been tracking down the Prince of the Indies, who, according to our prisoners, was wearing a slave's armor.

At the end of the third day we came across a group of warriors whose clothes were in shreds and whose horses were bleeding. They moved in a particular way that attracted Alexander's attention: he gave a great cry and carved a path for himself with his lance, swooping eagle-like on a slave who rode in the middle of the formation of Indians. The two men eyed each other. Both had bandaged wounds and had lost their helmets. Their faces were daubed with mud and blood, and the only thing alive in them was their glowering, shining eyes. They stared at each other for a moment as if each hoped he might kill his enemy with the ferocity and pride in his eyes; then they threw themselves at each other, screaming.

Alexander's sword wounded Poros's arm, and two Indian warriors came to help their master. They surrounded Alexander, and Poros ran away, but the king threw off his attackers and set off in pursuit of his prey. I let go of a man I was about to kill and rejoined Alexander in his headlong gallop. We followed Poros deep into a part of the forest that had not been burned. The sun was sinking, and this made Alexander nervous. Afraid that Poros might slip through his fingers at nightfall, he redoubled the pace and rushed into a circular meadow. Suddenly high-pitched whistling sounds rose up and interrupted the thunder of our horses' hooves. Arrows aimed at us were flying from the surrounding trees.

Poros had set a trap for Alexander! Alexander the invincible, too eager to finish off his rival, too impatient to claim victory, had offered himself to his enemy's archers! But it was too late to think. We surrounded the king and made a wall with our bodies. I waved my daggers to deflect the arrows, but in vain: they embedded themselves in my legs. A muffled cry made me shudder, and I turned to see that Alexander, who already had several arrows in him, had one right in the middle of his forehead. He fell from his horse. I slipped to the ground and dragged myself painfully toward him. Blood was spreading over his forehead, down his nose, and onto his pale cheeks. Blood spilled into my eyes, and something knocked me out.

When I came around, it was already night. The arrows had stopped whistling. Shadowy figures moved closer to us, cooing with joy in a language that sounded like strange night birds. We had been taken prisoner by Poros.

. . .

I WOKE IN the dark to the *boom-boom* of drums, and realized straight away that my hands and feet were tied. A long time went by before I remembered what had happened: Alexander's body had been taken away; the surviving soldiers had been piled onto carts and taken to Poros's encampment, where we were searched from head to foot. The Indian soldiers cried in amazement when they discovered I was a woman. Their officer left. When he returned, he gave the order to carry me to a tent, where two women hauled out the arrows that had struck me, and I passed out with the pain.

I crawled to the side of the tent and put my eye up to a gap: I could see the soldiers guarding me and campfires blazing in the distance. The sound of singing and clapping reached me, and there were silhouettes dancing round the fires—Poros was celebrating his victory.

Where was Alexander? Where were the soldiers? Where was Alestria?

I woke again when dawn lit up the tent and shed light over my body, which was wrapped in Indian cloth. Some women came in and untied me, took off my bandages, and changed the foul damp mud applied to my wounds. They gave me some food, then tied me up. They came back toward the end of the day. A little later night fell, and in the distance, the celebrations began once more. I felt no fear and no regret. I was expecting torture, rape, and execution—that is the fate reserved for the defeated. For a warrior there is no humiliation in this, it is the natural end to a fight.

Toward the middle of the next day some men burst into the tent, tipped me violently onto a carved wooden door, tied me to it, gagged me, and carried me out of the tent. Trees skimmed past me against the sky. I greeted passing birds, asking them to fly to my queen and my sisters, and tell them Ania would be joining the glorious souls of the warrior women.

There were four men carrying me on their shoulders, and they were joined by an escort of horsemen. Shouting and jeering started up, accompanied by slow, languid music. We passed foot soldiers, more horsemen, and then Poros on his golden chariot or—more likely—one of his look-alikes.

Some westerners on horseback loomed against the sky. They slipped to the ground and leaned over me. I recognized Hephaestion! The Indians put me down and withdrew, while the Macedonian soldiers untied me and took the gag from my mouth.

"Alexander!" I cried. "Where is Alexander?"

I leaped to my feet, but a sharp pain shot through me, and I fell back down.

"Alexander has gone home," Hephaestion replied.

His words chilled me to the bone: so Alexander was dead.

The soldiers helped me to a sedan chair. Alexander's troops greeted me as I passed before them. I could not help shedding tears when I spotted the royal tent adorned with gold and pearls gleaming at the far end of an avenue guarded by soldiers. Four Amazons took over my chair, lifted the door of the tent, and set me down inside.

Alestria was standing, while Alexander, stretched out on a wooden door like mine, still had the arrow that had brought him down in his forehead.

"Alexander is not dead. You, Ania, have come back to me! I am the happiest woman in the world," the queen told me, smiling, as tears welled in her eyes and spilled down her cheeks and onto her husband's arm.

. . .

POROS KNEW THAT if he killed Alexander, the Macedonians and Persians would come back to avenge their king's death. He also knew that the arrow that had struck Alexander's forehead was fatal.

Alexander was still alive, but he was condemned to die.

Poros had proposed peace to the Macedonians in exchange for their king's body.

Hephaestion had negotiated with Poros and promised to leave Indian territory.

Hephaestion and Poros had agreed on the division of wealth: the Macedonians would leave Poros any towns conquered in the Indies, while Poros would hush up Alexander's injury and capture, and would help put about the word that Alexander was still alive.

Poros's army withdrew.

Alexander's army erected a wall of spikes around the encampment.

Hephaestion transported Alexander's body inside a sealed tent. He purified the air by burning large candles. He delicately removed the arrowhead using a magnetic stone, closed the hole in the skull with powdered ivory, and covered the wound with skin taken from Alexander's leg. Alexander lay in darkness for three days. His heart was beating, but he did not talk or even open his eyes.

Alestria, alone in her tent, could not eat. She lay with her eyes closed, not sleeping but praying.

. . .

FLAMES PRESS AGAINST each other, joining together and then exploding. Flames crawl and leap and swirl. They are black, threatening, ice-cold. I stray aimlessly through the world of flames, not knowing who I am. I move forward and turn back. I run and then walk. Who am I? I finger a body I do not know but which is somehow mine.

The flames throw themselves at me, then drop back and fall to the ground. I am not afraid. They seem familiar to me. They are like me. They have come to cheer me on with their frenetic dancing.

A question hovers over my lips.

"Do you have souls?" I ask them.

A sharp pain stabs at me. The flames quiver, try to strangle me, then withdraw, and I understand that this is a forbidden question in this world. By asking it, I have proved I have a soul. Whose is it?

Every part of me hurts, and I curl up tightly. I roll on the ground, then leap to my feet and start to run. But the pain follows me. The pain is inside my body, so the soul is also rooted in my body. The flames leer and sneer at me. They are the damned whose souls have been taken; that is why they seem so voracious and so fierce, and why they do not burn me. For, without souls, all beings are but illusion. They can survive only thanks to the fear they engender.

I have a soul. I am Alexander! That name is a terrible aching! Images reel by in the flames.

Two little boys going into Apollo's temple. The marble god watches them as they undress and fall into each other's arms.

A woman with a long braid and heavy breasts leans on the balustrade of a terrace, waving her hand and weeping.

A city appears with painted walls, embroidered flags, and streets milling with people and horses. A succession of palaces, and in them eunuchs and concubines.

Muddy roads, torrential rains, icy tracks, unbearable cold! Corpses slither over the flames, wearing different costumes, bearing open wounds. Columns of smoke rise up and wither away. Breached ramparts, sumptuous banquets, and warriors' faces all file by. Fruits and vegetables spring from the gaping neck of a bull. Naked men embracing women wrapped in fine cloth, swaying together and disappearing. All these images make up Alexander. Alexander is mountains climbed, rivers crossed, land burned. Alexander is in the dust, in the clouds, and in the ashes.

A voice calls me: "Alexander, Alexander!"

It is a woman's voice. I do not know her: she is pure and tender, it is not my mother's anxious voice, no, it is not my mother—she is far away, I fled from her, she can no longer reach me, hold me to her breasts, kiss my forehead, stroke my hair, put me to bed, or laugh and weep about my fate. This woman is different; her voice is simple and courageous, she loves me and wants nothing from me. She is looking for me and calling to me to take me back to another world, where I will be delivered from these flames and illusions.

What is her name? Where did I meet her? How did she find me among the flames? These questions will never have answers. But what use are answers? I must follow her, I must trust her. Alexander has been defeated.

An arrow hurtles toward me and plants itself violently in the middle of my forehead. The flames go out, and I fly through the blue transparent universe, twirling toward the light, my heart brimming with joy. I smile, every portion of my body smiles, and I can hear the universe smile. I am in another world, one the flames cannot reach. Solemn music resonates through me and through the clarity of each ray of light.

White lights form a gigantic door. I move closer, a tiny body longing to receive life, waiting for the door to open for the distribution of souls.

The door metamorphoses into a face surrounded by a golden halo. It reminds me of Philip, my father, but this man has both his eyes. His eyes are open, clear blue; he has no wrinkles or scars. All earthly suffering has been erased from this face, it radiates with goodness. This must be a god who has taken on my father's appearance in order to address me.

"Go back to the earth," he tells me. "Your destiny has not finished being written. Go back, oh body without a soul, go back to your soul that stayed below for the love of a woman."

I bow to him and hurry away, tumbling through the air. The wind whistles, blue turns to white, and the white grows dark. I scatter, reassemble myself, then break again. I fall headlong, spinning downward.

I opened my eyes. The candle flames flickered.

A man sat up sharply and leaped out of the tent.

"The king is alive! The king has opened his eyes!"

Cheering broke out. Men filed past the table I was lying on: I recognized Hephaestion, Cassander, Bagoas, and all my companions. They withdrew, and silence returned. A woman came in, lifted one corner of her veil, and leaned over me. Her lips were cool. I drank her breath like water, I drank her life like honey. She put her arms around me, and I entered into her as a gazelle leaps into a spring river.

Alestria—I came back for her!

CHAPTER 11

Glory, wealth, and war were no longer of interest to me. The crimson tunic embroidered with three phoenixes that Bagoas helped me into and the golden wreath Hephaestion put on my head no longer thrilled me. Military formations, gleaming lances, harnessed horses, and the hundreds of thousands of men beating their shields and crying in unison, "Alexander! Alexander! Alexander!" . . . all of it bored me. Like a man who has been physically gratified, like a hero who has accomplished his exploits, like Ulysses back in his own country, what I had been through no longer interested me.

I let Hephaestion lead me and leaned on Bagoas. I made the effort to stand upright, but the sun dazzled me, the wind chilled me to the bone, and military parades left me anxious. I was happier in the darkness beneath my tent. The silence soothed my headaches but diffused them all over my body. Hephaestion gave me a drug to ease my pain, but it made me drowsy, so he gave me another to keep me awake. In our council meetings the generals debated and argued, calling on Alexander to arbitrate: I simply smiled at them.

I remembered our campaign in snatches. I understood nothing of their discussions, and their impassioned reasoning struck me as ridiculous or boring in turns. I said nothing, had lost the use of my tongue. Alexander, the peerless orator, could no longer utter a single coherent sentence. I could not wait to get back to my tent and lie down.

The passing days and various journeys were like flocks of birds scattering. I had neither the desire nor the strength to catch any of them. To demonstrate to the soldiers that Alexander had recovered, Hephaestion organized two attacks and arranged for them to be led by two men who looked like me. Then, urged on by the generals, he ordered a retreat. From the depths of my tent I heard Hephaestion's words as he gave me an account of our position. He hopped from one foot to the other, turned circles, and spewed great spates of indignant words and exalted speeches. His despair and his bellicose excesses left me unmoved. I had absolutely no response to these futile events. I tried to communicate how I felt to him by smiling at him broadly: he sighed and withdrew.

In Hephaestion's eyes, I had been strong and I had grown weak. I could no longer fight or even think.

In my own eyes, I had been weak and had grown strong. Hatred, frustration, jealousy, fear of being bettered, terror of being defeated . . . all these had disappeared. The bustle of this earthly world could no longer affect me. I had stopped suffering it. I was living.

A woman came to me. She lay over me when my headaches made me moan, and her skin cooled me, her silence lulled me. She kissed me and caressed me. Even though I could not feel her touch, I experienced a sense of well-being from head to foot.

A wall had grown up between myself and other men. We now marched in two different worlds.

I could not say whether Alestria slipped into my universe or I, Alexander, penetrated hers. I read her thoughts, heard her music, and let myself be carried away by her dreams. Alestria, take me home to your land!

. . .

ALEXANDER HAD TERRIBLE headaches that confined him to a darkened tent. Hephaestion gave him infusions to ease the pain, and the king slept even when his eyes were open. He could no longer fight, said nothing, and could only walk if he leaned on two guards. His hand could not find his mouth: it was Alestria who fed him. But Hephaestion, Cassander, Ptolemy, and Perdiccas needed Alexander to rule over his empire. They had agreed to put a look-alike on the throne. To give the lie credibility, they had made their peace with Bagoas: the eunuch's presence beside the false Alexander silenced any rumors.

The real king stayed closeted in the Amazons' quarters. Alestria refused to continue playing the role of Roxana, Queen of Asia, so Hephaestion had to find a look-alike for her too.

That night Alestria came into my tent and instructed me to

pack our things. In the flickering candlelight I was struck by her glowing red cheeks and shining eyes, and recognized the smile she had lost so long ago. Alestria slipped away, and I packed in feverish excitement. She did not tell me where we were going, but I, Ania, her faithful serving woman, knew.

I threw away the luxurious tunics, precious jewels, and embroidered sandals. I left aside the furniture, carpets, dishes, and incense. I lay down on the small bundle of bare essentials and fell asleep with a smile on my face.

When Alestria came to find me, it was still dark. All the girls of Siberia were standing outside their tents in battle costumes and with their horses ready. I carried Alexander and settled him in an Indian carriage with a roof over it. His monkey, Nicea, hurtled out of the tent, climbed onto his master's shoulder, and wrapped its arms round his head. Only Hephaestion came out; neither Bagoas, Cassander, nor Ptolemy was there to bid good-bye to their king. The two men looked at each other in silence for a long time, their eyes shining in the darkness. Hephaestion came over and laid his lips on Alexander's.

Alestria was at the head of our little troop, and she gave the signal to leave. I, Ania, was driving the chariot, and I urged my horses into a trot.

There, before the empty tents, Hephaestion stood like a figure turned to stone and was soon reduced to a smudge diluted by the night.

The gates to the encampment opened, and we, the Amazons, the daughters of the glacier, flew away.

. . .

HEPHAESTION HAD CHOSEN his fate and I mine.

Our kiss sealed it: I yielded Pella, Athens, Memphis, Babylon, Suse, Ecbatana, and the countless Alexandrias to him. Let him have the burden of the empire. Let me have a new life.

The roads carved out by Alexander the Great twisted and climbed and wound back down again. Caravans created clouds of dust, and soldiers patrolled up and down. Garrisons the size of a whole village took us in for the night, mistaking us for humble traders. The officers there led a debauched life, surrounded by slaves, prostitutes, and courtesans. The soldiers drank so much through the night that they were still drunk in the morning. We moved on, getting away from their rowdy bustle, and rode through the mountains for days. I listened to birdsong and the whisper of waterfalls. The valleys were carpeted with wild flowers, I could no longer smell their fragrance, but they touched my heart. My body swam in a limpid lake; my skin quivered. We reached the plain, with its tall grasses and ever-shifting clouds. I let myself be tied to my wife with a wide belt, my arms around her waist and my head on her shoulder. She urged on her horse, and I galloped with her. The wind whistled, and the sun burst into showers of golden light. I felt so tall my head skimmed the very sky, and my feet made the earth shake beneath them.

An army appeared on the horizon: warriors in helmets raising their bows. The women around me could not contain their joy. Ania was heading up our little troop, and she galloped toward them like an arrow. The soldiers threw their helmets in the air, dropped from their horses, and ran toward Alestria. As they jostled to touch my wife's legs and feet, I realized they were actually young women. Alestria jumped down, and the girls milled round her, kissing her and raising her high in the air. Then they followed her over to my carriage and peered at me curiously, touching my hair and shoulders and chattering with excitement. They picked up my monkey, who struggled to break free, screaming in fear. This made the girls laugh, and their laughter washed through me like a warm current. My every muscle relaxed, and first I smiled, then drew my lips right open and burst out laughing.

"Alexander is laughing!" Ania cried in Persian. "He has recovered!"

Alestria ran over to me, looked at me, and wept with joy.

· · ·

ALESTRIA'S TRIBE LIVED to the rhythm of good pastureland. The girls rose with the dawn and went to sleep when the sun set. They shared all forms of manual work and took turns putting on armor to fight as warriors. They laughed and sang a great deal. They gave Nicea a small horse and taught him to gallop, and they trained some gray mice to make a circus for my entertainment. On feast days they gathered round the campfire in the evenings and drank alcohol made from flower roots; then they became even more cheerful and playful, dancing like will-o'-the-wisps. I joined in their games and gradually regained the use of my hands. By concentrating on every note, I managed a form of singing and pronounced a few simple words.

On our travels we found little girls abandoned by their parents, while young warrior women with barely a wrinkle on their faces would leave us to go and die. These young women knew from the stars when the end had come for them. They took a potion that numbed them to pain and left on horseback without telling anyone. When the horse returned to camp alone a few days later, it signaled a period of mourning. Ania explained that the Amazon would ride until she saw a river, then she would dismount and lie down on the bank. She would let vultures and other scavengers eat her body while her soul rose up to the skies to become a star.

And so it was that, reading the constellation in the vault of the sky, Alestria decided to take me on a journey. Spring had come round again. We set off, following the wild geese, with Alestria riding beside me, Ania driving my chariot, and Nicea on my shoulder. Every morning the reddening sun rose, and every evening the moon waxed larger. We came across a whole army of caribou with massive antlers, hundreds of thousands of them, surging toward the north. Our little stream joined that great river, and it bore us along in its frenetic galloping.

The tall grasses disappeared, succeeded by dry earth covered in pebbles and bare rock. A dark line of trees stretched out on the horizon. Still surrounded by the caribou, which never stopped to rest, we penetrated deep into a forest of pine, tall and upright as lances. A few days later some warriors blocked our way. They had black hair adorned with feathers and wore animal skins sewn with shells.

Alestria went over toward them and came back to me with a beaming smile on her face.

"The Great Mother is expecting us!" she cried. "She read in the stars that the queen had returned with the king."

Caribou led up ahead and followed on behind, while these new warriors escorted us. Having crossed a wide, shallow river,

I came for the first time to the land of the volcano, where birds and stags came to drink and sing their song. The Great Mother, queen of the People of the Volcano, came to greet us in a chariot pulled by dogs with blue and yellow eyes. She led us through her kingdom, a series of villages scattered about a vast plain that sloped down toward the ocean.

The sea wind whipped up blue-black waves, and on the horizon, I could see a chain of white glaciers. A flock of birds wheeled above, calling, then diving down into the water and reappearing with fish in their beaks. All at once gray monsters with great wide jaws emerged from the waves, spewing jets of water that shimmered with rainbows as they fell back down.

The People of the Volcano constituted a tribe governed by the Great Mother. They elected their queen from among the women who had had many children, who had, in turn, produced many grandchildren. Unlike the Amazons, who disliked old age, the People of the Volcano only trusted those who reached a great age. The Great Mother had blue tattoos on her cheeks and a beard on her chin. Alestria told me that the women of the volcano lived a long time; hence their wisdom and their gift for reading the stars. But the Great Mother did not decide anything: every full moon she held feasting during which the village chiefs would have their discussions. She would put in a word only if there were disagreements.

We waited for winter to return and cover the ocean with thick ice; then we spread grease over our bodies and wrapped ourselves in warm furs. We packed away our tents and utensils onto the sleds pulled by dogs. With the Great Mother up at the front and the entire tribe behind her, we launched ourselves onto that white continent, facing into the wind and the snow.

As we slid on, I forgot to count off the days. The sun had disappeared behind the glaciers and no longer rose. Beams of green, orange, purple, and white light carved through that endless night, tearing open the black sky. Wolves howled in the distance, setting off furious barking competitions among the dogs. Nicea wriggled beneath my coat and shrieked with them.

White bears sitting on blocks of ice watched us pass. Silvery foxes flitted across the snow and hid behind large white rocks. The People of the Volcano hunted hares and creatures with thick fatty skin and bristly mustaches and that, when glimpsed in the distance, looked like mermaids.

A black volcano with a glowering red summit loomed through the misty darkness. Soon I could make out its lava flow: scarlet waves and crimson sparks edging down its flanks and spilling into the sea. We camped on the red and black rock, dotted with patches of snow. The men set to work extracting blocks of metal from mines and transporting them to the foot of the volcano. On the other side, where the earth's blood flowed, a series of reservoirs had been dug into the slopes as well as canals to deflect the lava. By opening successive sluice gates, the People of the Volcano made the incandescent flows run over metal positioned in the upper reservoirs. They directed the molten metal toward reservoirs lower down, and these in turn spewed the red-hot liquid into molds in the shape of swords, bludgeons, and sickles.

The women gathered the tarnished black blades, beat them out, and dunked them in the snow. The Great Mother led these ceremonies, invoking the souls of warriors of the glacier to be incarnated into these weapons, which grew light, razor-sharp, and indestructible. So it was that the Amazon girls had been able to fight men since time immemorial. So it was that Alestria had broken through Alexander's shield when we confronted each other for the first time.

We returned to the land mass when spring came round again.

The Great Mother pronounced an oracle, and the men started cutting down pine trees and building boats. The women went down onto the beach and dug in the sand with their weapons, creating a wide channel sloping up the beach. The gray whales, great floating islands bearing whole populations of shellfish and seaweed on their backs, resurfaced and dazed us with their wailing song. Summer returned, and caribou spread throughout the kingdom. On the day singled out by the God of Ice, the men launched their vessels on the sea. In among the whales they found the queen with red and yellow markings, and they threw spears and stones at her.

The whales were quick-tempered. When their queen was angry, she spewed columns of water and stirred up giant waves that overturned the boats. But the People of the Volcano carried on harrying her. Maddened with rage, she gave chase to her attackers, setting off up the channel and throwing herself onto the shore.

The death throes of the queen of the ocean were accompanied by celebrations. Out among the waves the other whales circled, singing their mournful song for many days and nights before electing a new queen and heading off toward the south. The whale meat was salted and kept for lean years. Her skin became roofing for huts; her grease, oil for lamps; and her bones, pillars bleached by the wind, formed a gigantic alleyway along which, I was told, the God of Ice would come.

Autumn came round again. The grasses turned yellow and dried out, the birds flew south, and the caribou set off once more. On clear evenings when the stars twinkled in the sky, the Great Mother stood by the fire and sang:

The Amazons, the whales, and the People of the Volcano
Are descended from Mount Siberia.

Our god created the glacier.
Our land warmed up.
The glacier became a mountain.
Then the snows fell.
The wintry mountain became the glacier again.
The glacier dissolved and turned into a lake.
The lake disappeared when a volcano rose up.

The mountain clan had descendants.
Two peoples crossed the ocean.
We no longer know their history.
Three species of birds fled the great freeze.
Five species of flower came down to earth.
Infinite are the warrior spirits wandering the skies.
Infinite are our invisible sisters who return to our bodies and souls.

The Amazons will disappear.
The People of the Volcano will die out.
The whales will cease to sing.
The black weapons will be forgotten.
But warrior souls shall carry on.

I, Alexander, the warrior from the other side of the mountain, could not feel my queen's gentle caress. I could not tell her how much I loved her. I drank in her body, embraced her soul, lived in her eyes, in her laughter, in her happiness at having me by her side.

When the migraines struck me, she lay over me, and her cool skin soothed the blazing pain.

I spoke to her with my trembling hands. I loved her with my heart, which fought against death for her sake. I had offered her war, kingdoms, and endless traveling; she had offered me whales, white cranes, and a volcano spewing the blood and ash of life.

Come with me, Alestria. Let us fly toward the light shining down from the glacier.

Come with me, my queen. Let us fly toward the sun.

Come with me, invincible soul. Let us fly toward the centuries that shall sing forever of our names, our exploits, and our glory.

· · ·

ALEXANDER AND HIS monkey were always cold, so we wrapped them in thick layers of fur.

Alexander had difficulty speaking. He could not feel when he was being touched. But with simple gestures he told me how grateful he was to the arrow that had transformed his fate.

Alexander and Alestria held hands and spent their time looking at the glaciers. They woke to watch the sunrise and gazed in rapture at the sunset.

Alexander and Alestria loved each other intensely for thirty-six moons. Alexander left one morning in spring. Alestria came back to the steppes with me and dictated these words to me in the language of birds.

Alestria disappeared one morning, and her horse returned.

I, Ania, the faithful serving girl of the queen of the Amazons, wrote the end of this book. The following day I rose at dawn. I drank the potion prepared the day before and gave some to Nicea to drink. He climbed onto my shoulder, and I walked out of the tent.

I urged my horse into a gallop. Following my queen's instructions, I shall bury these pages of stone in a cave. I shall close the mouth of the cave.

I shall stop when we come to a river.

There is a white eagle in the sky.

Guiding me to the summit.

To you, boy child of the future, I give these words written in the
  language of birds,
To you, intrepid warrior, I give our freedom and our galloping,
Watch over our sleeping,
Watch over our seasons.

To you, young girl who reads the stars,
To you, young girl who deciphers the book of birds,
To you, little girl who fears neither suffering nor death,

I give the secret of our souls,
The secret of love,
The secret of strength.